THE
INSIDE
BATTLE

THE

INSIDE BATTLE

Melanie Sumrow

 YELLOW JACKET

YELLOW JACKET
an imprint of Little Bee Books

251 Park Avenue South, New York, NY 10010
Text copyright © 2020 by Melanie Sumrow
All rights reserved, including the right of
reproduction in whole or in part in any form.
Yellow Jacket and associated colophon are
imprints of Little Bee Books.
Manufactured in China TPL 0320
First Edition

10 9 8 7 6 5 4 3 2 1

Library of Congress Cataloging-in-Publication Data
Names: Sumrow, Melanie, author.
Title: The inside battle / Melanie Sumrow.
Description: First edition. | New York, NY: Yellow Jacket, [2020]
Summary: Longing for his father's approval, thirteen-year-
old Rebel Mercer follows him inside a racist, anti-government
militia group, but when his father plans an attack on an
African-American church, Rebel must make the most
important decision in his life. | Identifiers: LCCN 2019014014
Subjects: | CYAC: Militia movements—Fiction. | Post-traumatic stress
disorder—Fiction. | Veterans—Fiction. | Prejudices—Fiction. | Fathers
and sons—Fiction. | Courage—Fiction. | BISAC: JUVENILE
FICTION / Social Issues / Prejudice & Racism. |
JUVENILE FICTION / Family / General
(see also headings under Social Issues).
Classification: LCC PZ7.1.S857 In 2019 | DDC [Fic]—dc23
LC record available at https://lccn.loc.gov/2019014014

ISBN 978-1-4998-0917-6
yellowjacketreads.com

For information about special discounts on bulk purchases,
please contact Little Bee Books at sales@littlebeebooks.com.

To Mom, for encouraging me to find my voice

In honor of veterans and their families, for your many sacrifices

In the end, we will remember not the words of our enemies, but the silence of our friends.

—Dr. Martin Luther King, Jr.

ONE

They say the apple doesn't fall far from the tree, so I guess that makes me an orange. I'm nothing like my dad.

"Rebel," Aunt Birdie says gently. "I told you to get your father." She slides a pan back and forth on the cooktop as she fries bacon. It sizzles and pops, the smoky smell filling our kitchen. I drop my chocolate Pop-Tart onto my plate. Maybe if I loaded up on more protein, I'd get muscles like Dad's.

I flex my left arm and squeeze my scrawny bicep with my other hand.

Aunt Birdie laughs when she sees what I'm doing.

My arm drops to my side. "One more time?" I ask, pulling my robot, a rectangular-shaped block, backward until he touches the newspaper. "You know how Dad *hates* QUEN-10."

Dad's a Marine—an actual American hero—and he got

home from Afghanistan several months ago. Or, really, the government sent him home. He likes things the way he likes them.

"One more," my aunt says, returning her focus to the browning bacon. I set the timer on my watch and release my robot.

QUEN-10, who's a little wider than a Pop-Tart with quarter-sized wheels, rolls across our kitchen table. "Come on," I say as he passes the saltshaker. It doesn't look like he's going to stop, but then he makes an abrupt right-angle turn, avoiding the jar of grape jelly. I smile. He's working.

I check my watch and finish my milk. "Come on," I say again, wiping the wet mustache from my upper lip with the back of my hand.

The shovel attachment on QUEN-10 drops with a whizzing sound and then scoops a small plastic disc from the table and flips it over. "Yes!" My robot slides the disc next to the target area—the tub of butter—to bring my starting score to twenty-five points.

Aunt Birdie sets a plate of toast on the end of the table. "Time's up, kid."

QUEN-10 glides in reverse and returns to home base—the newspaper. I stop the timer. "If I'm going to get more points than Ajeet, I have to make sure I can finish at least eight missions in under two-and-a-half minutes."

Aunt Birdie hovers, drumming her glittery nails on the table. "I thought you guys were BFFs."

I don't even try to hide my eye-roll. I turned thirteen a few weeks ago and now my aunt thinks she's cool when she uses "teen speak" on me.

She puts her hands on her hips, covering BB-8 on the Star Wars scrubs I gave her last Christmas. She's trying to pretend she's angry, but then smiles. "Don't give me that look, young man. I know you know what BFF means."

"Right," I whisper so Dad doesn't hear. "Ajeet and I are friends."

She gives me a knowing nod. "Your dad's taking you to school today."

My shoulders tense.

"It'll be okay," she says, giving me a pat on the back. "Now clean this up and go get him for me."

I turn off QUEN-10 and lower him into the plastic crate next to my foot. My hand sweeps across the table, corraling the remaining Lego pieces before I drop them next to my robot.

"Your dad needs to eat his breakfast before that job

interview this morning." Aunt Birdie then lowers the pans into the sudsy sink water with a splash.

I quickly scan the table, making sure everything's in place, and nestle the saltshaker against the pepper before positioning them to the right of Dad's plate. "Who's he interviewing with this time?" My dad has survived five deployments to Iraq and Afghanistan. But he hasn't been able to land a job now that he's home in Amarillo, Texas.

Aunt Birdie sits in her chair across from me and bites into her crispy bacon. "It's that mechanic position down at the stockyards." She swallows and lowers her voice. "I think it'd be good for him. Might give him a healthier routine."

Dad doesn't like to talk about it, but he has a lot of bad memories from being a Marine, and they sneak up on him sometimes. "He'll get it," I say, trying to sound confident. I don't like seeing Aunt Birdie so worried. And lately, she worries a lot about Dad.

A weak smile crosses her face as she nods. "Go on. You know how he gets when he hasn't eaten his breakfast." She laughs, but it comes out sounding sad.

I stand and approach the wooden bench that sits beneath our coat pegs, trying my best to ignore the bug-out bags Dad makes us keep lined along the floor in case of an apocalypse or government attack.

After placing my crate on the bench, I hurry down the long hallway, my steps muffled by the thick carpet. Our house belonged to my grandparents before they died. First my grandma, followed by my grandpa a month later. Aunt Birdie says he died of a broken heart, and since she's a nurse, I believe her.

The walls still hold the same pictures of my aunt and Dad with them getting older and taller as you move down the hallway.

At the end, there's a picture of Dad, standing in front of a tank with his platoon. He looks like a hero from one of those war movies. It was taken when he was in Iraq the first time. I was about two then.

I bite my lip and face the door to the basement. There's a KEEP OUT sign taped to it, but I knock anyway.

No response.

With my ear against the door, I try knocking again. "Dad?"

Still silence.

The door always sticks, so with one hand on the knob and my shoulder against the door, I push it open with a *pop* and stumble forward a bit. There's a dim light coming from the basement, but the wood-paneled wall blocks my view. "Dad?"

Nothing.

My fingertips slip across the flats and grooves in the paneling as I carefully descend the steep, carpeted steps.

As soon as I reach the floor, I can see that his bed is made like he's ready for someone to inspect it. He's dressed, but sits with his back to me. A white glow beams from his computer, highlighting the yellow flag with the rattlesnake that hangs above his desk.

I clear my throat, but he doesn't turn around. The picture of Mom, the one where she's laughing at Cadillac Ranch, sits on the desk to his left. It was taken a few months before she died.

To his right, I spot the handgun—the one he keeps loaded. My chest tightens. I really wish he didn't have that thing.

He's typing vigorously and, from the black sun and moon at the top of the screen, I can tell he's chatting with that militia group again: the Flag Bearers.

My fingers curl against my legs as I look to the right, where Dad has spent the last few months re-creating a battle scene on top of Grandma's old Ping-Pong table with toy soldiers, plastic tanks, and sand. He's even used cotton to mimic the smoke coming from a conquered city.

"Don't touch it," Dad barks, startling me.

I didn't even realize he'd turned around. He's pretty stealth like that. The muscles in his arms and chest bulge beneath his cotton dress shirt. I raise my hands, as if surrendering. "I—I didn't."

From the light of the computer, I can see his clothes are pressed, but there's still a shadow of stubble across his cheeks. He rubs his eyes. They're red, which probably means he didn't get any sleep again. Some nights, I can hear him pacing the house for hours.

He sighs; his muscles relax. "I'm sorry, bud. You startled me."

"Breakfast is ready," I say, thumbing toward the stairs.

Dad stares at me for a second, and suddenly, it feels like I'm the one being inspected. His eyes linger on my planetarium T-shirt before moving to my long, skinny legs and down to my running shoes that never run. I can tell he's disappointed as usual.

"Aunt Birdie made eggs," I say past the lump in my throat.

"I've got to finish this email." He spins around, facing his computer. Immediately, his back stiffens. Dad curses and slams his fist against the desk, making the gun skitter across the surface. I jump as he starts pounding the keyboard again.

Forget it, I'll just walk to school. I retreat up the stairs, taking them two at a time.

As I return to the kitchen, Aunt Birdie glances past me. "Where's your dad?"

I'm a little winded from the stairs, but manage a shrug. "Busy?"

Her face twists as she snaps her fingers. "No, sir. He's not doing this to me today."

"I can walk," I offer, begging her with my eyes: *Please don't make me ask him again.*

And it works. Kind of. She stomps past me, her Crocs thudding along the hallway. "Nathan," she calls to the basement.

My fingers twist the bottom of my T-shirt. I hope Dad doesn't think I sent her.

"Breakfast is ready. You've got that interview this morning," she says. "And you need to take your son to school."

"Just give me a second!" Dad shouts.

I cringe.

"We don't have a second," Aunt Birdie answers. "You know I'm helping with that root canal this morning, and Rebel needs to get to school on time."

I lift my backpack from the peg and sling the strap over my shoulder. "Really, I can walk," I say as she enters the kitchen.

"Carrying all of your robotics stuff?" She shakes her head.

I nod and my foot accidentally knocks into one of Dad's bug-out bags. He's assembled one for each of us—a black backpack filled with dehydrated food, dry matches, a hunting knife, and more stuff I don't know how to use. The bag tips away from my foot, but thankfully nothing falls out.

"Fine, I'm here," Dad says to Aunt Birdie as he brushes past me. I scramble to straighten the tipped backpack. He scowls; my hand comes off the bag. "Didn't I tell you I'd be up?"

I nod. "Yes, sir." Even though he didn't.

The legs of his chair scrape against the tile floor before he sits and snatches his fork, jabbing it toward his sister. "You're worse than a drill sergeant." He stabs his scrambled eggs and stuffs them inside his mouth. After a few chews, his shoulders soften. "But you sure make a better breakfast," he says, savoring the bite in his mouth before he shovels in more eggs.

Aunt Birdie zips toward her jacket, snatching it from the peg, while I grab my spare-parts crate off the bench. You never know when you might need something in the heat of competition. Then I get the crate with QUEN-10 and stack it on top.

Out of nowhere, Aunt Birdie sneaks up on me and kisses my cheek.

"Hey," I protest, leaning away from her. With my hands so full, I can't wipe it off. "Not while I'm defenseless."

She grins. "Good luck today. And don't forget your jacket," she says, pointing to my *Man Vs Robot* hoodie hanging against the wall.

I wrinkle my nose. I hate how she still treats me like a baby. Like I don't know when to wear my jacket or when to brush. I run my tongue across my gritty teeth. Oops.

"He's not a baby," Dad mutters, his mouth half-full of toast. "You shouldn't treat him like one."

Aunt Birdie presses her lips together, like she's holding something in. Probably her favorite curse word.

I shrug. "The man's got a point?"

She shakes her head. "Rebel, you'll do great today," she says and hurries toward the front door, slamming it shut.

Dad startles. His face tightens when he realizes I saw him jump.

Suddenly, I wish Aunt Birdie was still here.

But then he forces a deep breath and wipes his mouth with a napkin. "I guess you're ready to hit the road, too, huh?"

My stomach churns Pop-Tart, milk, and nerves. I eye my jacket on the hook and decide against it. "Yes, sir," I say with a quick nod before following him.

Outside, the late-spring wind swirls around me. Goose bumps lift along my arms. I shiver and hope Dad doesn't notice.

Aunt Birdie toots her car horn and pulls away from our house with a wave. I wish she could drive me to school today.

She always knows what to say to help keep me calm before a big test or competition.

Dad sticks his head out the driver's-side window on his pickup. "You getting in or what?"

I hurry around the front of his spotless maroon truck, shrugging my shoulders to my ears, trying to keep my neck warm. There's a new sticker in the lower corner of Dad's windshield: PROUD MEMBER over a black sun and a moon with FLAG BEARERS at the bottom.

When did he get that?

The wind gusts and pushes me sideways. I gulp, trying to keep everything upright and my breakfast down. My hands are so full, I bumble to open the passenger-side door, trying not to scratch Dad's truck, while attempting to balance my crates.

I finally get the door open and sense Dad's frustration without even looking at him.

"Sorry," I say as I drop the crates and my backpack onto the floorboard and get in.

The truck's engine roars, along with the radio. Dad likes to listen to talk radio. On full volume. Some guy's griping about how we should close our country's borders to all foreigners because they're stealing the jobs of real, red-blooded Americans. Whatever that's supposed to mean.

I'd change the station—Aunt Birdie and I listen to oldies—but Dad won't let me. He moves his jaw side to side and rolls his thick neck, like he's trying to relax. "When does spring training start?" Dad asks over the radio. He slides the truck into gear; the engine rumbles as we speed down our street.

I shift when we take a right so fast, the tires squeal. I was kind of hoping to avoid this conversation. "Already did."

"What?" he shouts. Dad and basically everyone in west Texas thinks there's only one sport every boy—even the shrimpy ones—should play: football.

"It started a couple of months ago," I say a little louder.

Dad slides a stiff hand across the side of his dark crew cut. He turns left at the neighborhood park. A mom with a patterned headscarf is pushing her toddler on the swings. My hand grips the armrest. Dad's always been a bit prejudiced. But lately, it seems to have gotten so much worse. I hope he doesn't see the woman and say something cruel.

Thankfully, he doesn't seem to notice as he zooms past. I actually manage to breathe until he asks, "So why aren't you bringing workout clothes to school?"

I want to scream: *Because I stink at football! At anything that has to do with sports or using my body in any sort of coordinated way! Can't you see I didn't inherit your manly muscles or superhero strength?*

Instead, I mumble, "Robotics and football practice are at the same time."

"So do football," he says, like it's the obvious solution.

My armpits are getting sweaty. I hope the deodorant Aunt Birdie bought really does work like the commercial says: *when you need it most.* I clear my throat. "I'm already doing robotics."

Dad glances at QUEN-10 for a second before his eyes return to the road. "Aren't you getting a little too old to play with these toys?"

I wince.

"Look, I'm only trying to help you." He nods to himself. "The world's tough out there. You need to be competitive."

I move the vent with my hand, trying to get more air, but nothing comes out. "There's a competition this afternoon," I argue.

"A *toy* competition?" He zips through a stop sign. "You need to be tough. And football helps you with that. You want to be a winner, right?"

I shrug. "I guess."

"You *guess*?"

Not this again. Not today, when I'm already nervous

about the competition. I turn away from his glare and lean my forehead against the cool window, willing us to get to school already.

The radio host is still screaming about the "evils of immigrants." Dad lowers the volume. "You know, the government's been letting all these foreigners in."

Ugh. If I throw up, will he stop talking?

"And, if you're not careful, they're going to take over. We have to be ready."

It feels like I'm suffocating. My breath fogs the glass as we pass Ajeet's house on the corner and finally, *finally* reach the school.

But then I spot my best friend, nestling his robot between his jacket and shirt as he run-walks across the school's lawn.

"God, they really are everywhere." Dad points to Ajeet as he struggles against the wind.

The collar on my T-shirt suddenly feels too tight.

"Oh, look. He's got a toy, too," Dad says sarcastically. We come to a stop at the end of the carpool line. "Do you know him?"

I throw open the door. "Here's good," I mutter, wanting to escape.

"Hey, what are you doing?" Dad asks. "Let me pull up first."

"That's okay." I jump from the truck, scrambling to grab my backpack and crates. The wind blows against my back, drying my sweat. I force myself not to shiver as I jostle QUEN-10 and the parts box, and then elbow the door closed.

My eyes zero in on the school's entrance. I know it's wrong, but if I hurry, Dad won't see me talking to Ajeet. I rush along the sidewalk.

"Rebel," my friend calls.

Oh, no.

"Hey!" Ajeet's shoes glide across the grass, making a whooshing sound. "Wait up."

I go faster, but then he cuts me off. "You deaf or something? I'm talking to you."

My gaze drops to a crack in the sidewalk. "Uh, sorry."

"Rebel!"

My knees tremble at the sound of Dad's rough voice. He's still grasping the steering wheel with one hand while leaning toward the open passenger-side window.

Kids rush past us. "Is that your dad?" Ajeet asks and then waves. "Hi, Mr. Mercer!"

"What are you doing?" I say under my breath, pushing his hand down. Dad scowls. My heart beats fast. "Let's go inside."

My friend's eyebrows knit in confusion.

"Look at me," Dad barks. He's blocking the carpool line, but he doesn't care. "That's an order, young man!"

Ajeet's mouth falls open; my toes clench the insides of my shoes.

Cars honk as I follow Dad's order.

His face is red. "We are not finished here."

I want to shout: *Yes, we are!* I want to grab Ajeet by the shoulder and scream: *This is my friend; it shouldn't matter what he looks like!*

But I don't.

Like the coward I am, I turn and run.

TWO

So running away from Dad this morning wasn't one of my finest moments. It probably ranks only slightly better than the time when I was five and zoomed around in front of Mom's friends, wearing nothing but underwear on my head, yelling, *I'm Captain Cotton! I'm Captain Cotton!* Aunt Birdie still likes to bring that one up.

"Hey," Ajeet says. "You okay?" It's about the fiftieth time he's asked since I freaked on the sidewalk. School's almost out for the day, but I still haven't been able to stop thinking about it. I'll never be tough enough or anywhere near good enough for my dad.

The rubber soles on our shoes squeak against the waxed floors as we walk the long, empty hallway on the way to our school's gym. Our science teacher let us out a little early so we could grab our robotics crates from the tables in the gym and be ready to compete. Ajeet nudges me with his elbow. "Because if you want to talk ab—"

"I'm fine," I lie, cutting him off. Through the hand smears on the double glass doors, I spot the vans from other schools. My stomach bubbles with nerves. I need to focus.

Only two kids move on to Regionals, and one of them *has* to be me. I may not be any good at football. But maybe I can still prove to Dad that I can be a winner.

As we turn the corner, the school bell rings, signaling the end of the day. Ajeet and I both cover our ears and pick up the pace. Classroom doors fly open. My hands drop to my sides as we push through kids streaming from their classes, all chatter and laughter.

"Hey, Rebel," Connor says as he exits one of the classes with that cool wave of his. He's the star pitcher of our undefeated baseball team.

"Hey," I reply. He keeps moving the opposite direction, his crowd of fans behind him.

"I don't know why Connor won't talk to me," Ajeet says as we turn the corner. "Do you think he's a racist?"

My jaw tightens. "I'm sure that's not it. He probably didn't see you."

"So I'm invisible now," he says. "Like that's so much better."

Heat flickers through me. I shake my head. Ajeet can be so sensitive sometimes. "Let it go, okay?" My voice comes out harsher than I meant.

Ajeet flinches. "I was just asking."

I force myself to take a deep breath as we walk—*one, two*—and exhale—*one, two*. Like Mom taught me. A little calmer, I add, "We've got bigger things to worry about than Connor Green."

Metal lockers open and slam shut around us, but the quiet between Ajeet and me is intense. I shouldn't have shouted at him. I don't know why I get so angry sometimes.

"I'm sorry," I finally say as we reach the gym. "I shouldn't have yelled. I guess I'm just nervous about the competition."

We stop a second before going in. "You worry too much," Ajeet finally says.

"You don't think I should be worried?" I ask, giving him the side-eye. Ajeet's the most competitive person I know. Besides Dad, of course. "Has an alien invaded your body or something?"

Ajeet snort-laughs, breaking the tension a little. "No, I'm not talking about that," he says, pointing inside the gym.

A kid shows his robot to an adult. There's a cage around it. *Too bulky*, I think.

"No, it's . . ." Ajeet pauses for a second, bringing my

attention to his face. His expression is serious as he shrugs. "My dad's hard on me, too."

"Oh," I say, surprised. Suddenly, I don't know where to look; my gaze hovers on his vintage Atari T-shirt. "Um." I plunge my hands into my jeans pockets and rock backward on my heels, not really knowing what to say, either. Sure, he's my best friend, but we usually talk about robots, gaming, and the BIG debate: whether Star Wars or Star Trek is better.

Star Wars, duh.

"Okay." Ajeet awkwardly coughs. "It's time for me to slay your baby robot with my ingenious masterpiece."

I grin. "You. Wish."

Inside the gym, it smells like sweat, but there are no jocks today—only a bunch of us nerds and teachers scattered across the gym floor. The competition table, where we run our robots through the tasks, sits at center court. I check the projection screen near the entrance: There are about thirty competitors total. Ajeet's drawn the sixth run; mine is seventh.

Two people move on to Regionals. And we only get one run. My heart flip-flops.

Mrs. Fuentes, our school principal, waves as she approaches. She's wearing her usual black suit, along with a genuine smile. "Glad to see you made it, gentlemen." Her perfume smells like a rose garden.

"Thanks, Mrs. F.," I say, and then wait for Ajeet to respond. But he only stares at her with his mouth open. Like always.

He thinks Mrs. Fuentes looks like the lady from the *Wonder Woman* movie and gets a little tongue-tied anytime she even looks at him, much less speaks to him.

Mrs. Fuentes nods at Ajeet. "Can't wait to see what you came up with." In response, he makes a strange gurgling noise.

I'd laugh if he wasn't so pitiful.

"Uh, thanks," I say. She doesn't look like Wonder Woman to me, but Mrs. Fuentes is still pretty cool. She's the whole reason our school is hosting the competition in the first place. Her son used to do this when he was a kid, and now he's some kind of engineer at NASA.

Ajeet still isn't moving. It's like he's Han Solo frozen in carbonite. I clear my throat. "I guess we better get our robots."

Mrs. Fuentes steps aside. "Of course, don't let me keep you."

I slap Ajeet's shoulder, urging him forward. When we're

under the basketball net, I whisper, "You really need to get a grip."

He immediately nods. "I don't know what's wrong with me."

"I've been wondering the same thing literally for years."

"*Hey*," he protests, but laughs with me as we reach the table where we left our robots, along with my box of spare parts. After my meltdown.

Most of the other competitors have already gathered around the main table to watch the first run of the day.

Ajeet's robot sits next to mine. Without the attachments, it's bigger than QUEN-10, almost the size of a Kleenex box, and taller with its large, rubber tires about the size of coasters. "Nice wheels," I say.

"Thanks," Ajeet says, "I'm hoping they'll keep him running clean across the board."

A loud buzz sounds and echoes throughout the gym, signaling the end of the first run. Two-and-a-half minutes go fast.

I glance over my shoulder as everyone cheers. The short kid who finished his run high-fives a tall, gangly girl. I check the score on the screen: 115. That's out of a total of 400. Good, but not good enough to win.

"You're smart to invert the motor," Ajeet says.

My chin lifts with pride. I knew he'd notice. My inverted motor is what makes QUEN-10 more compact and, hopefully, more agile.

I pick up my parts box and robot. There are two practice boards on the floor, where the organizers have re-created the competition table. There's one on each side of the gym. "Should we take them for a test run?" I ask, wanting to see my friend's robot in action.

A girl with a unicorn T-shirt has taken the practice board closest to us. Her robot pulls the plastic tower's handle, releasing Lego pieces at the base. The robot then drags the pieces with a claw attachment into the designated circle on the board. That task is worth sixty points. Not bad.

"Coming?" Ajeet asks, already halfway across the gym. The practice board on the other side is empty.

As I pass the main table, most of the competitors bite their nails and then erupt in cheers as they watch another run.

"You first," Ajeet says when I reach him. We sit on the floor next to the practice board.

I wipe my hands on my jeans. "Okay, I'll probably run the last program, since it's the newest." After shifting my weight to my knees, I push the gray buttons on QUEN-10, shuffling through my programs to the final one. When I've found it, I pull him to home base and press start. QUEN-10's wheels spin across the table to the opposite end before he makes a sudden forty-five-degree turn and stops short of a vertical wall.

"You're kidding," Ajeet says with a goofy grin. "You actually got this program to work?"

I cross my fingers and watch as QUEN-10 climbs the vertical wall using the claw. It makes a whizzing sound and then hooks onto the top. Yes!

"Whoa!" Ajeet says, his hands grabbing the sides of his head. "Mind's officially blown."

I sit a little taller.

"You're going to win, for sure. That's eighty points!"

"We'll see," I say, hoping he's right as I scoot along the floor to retrieve QUEN-10 from the wall. "Now let's see what your hunk of junk can do."

Ajeet scoots around the table to home base and lowers his robot onto the board. He presses the down button, sorting through his programs, until he finds the one he wants. With a tap, the large wheels move straight ahead and then, out of nowhere, veer left and into the tower, making some of its pieces drop to the board.

I cringe as the wheels on Ajeet's robot spin and groan but go nowhere.

His hands grip his knees. "Holy. Stephen. *Hawking*!" That's Ajeet's ridiculous attempt at cursing, putting "holy" in front of a famous scientist's name.

Cheers erupt at the main table.

I resist the temptation to check the latest score; Ajeet's nervous energy is starting to pierce my shaky calm. "It's okay," I say, trying to keep us both cool as I reassemble the tower. "Try again."

Ajeet bites his bottom lip and pulls his robot to home base. He checks to make sure he's selected the right program and then releases his robot. But it veers left again, crashing into a plastic barricade. "Holy *Galileo*!" he says, panic streaking his voice. "What am I going to do? They're already on the fourth run."

Think, think. What's a quick fix? It's veering, which means his gyro sensor's probably off. "Change the gyro?" I suggest.

He promptly shakes his head. "I don't have an extra. I spent all my money on these wheels." Then he spots the crate on my lap. "Do you have one?"

My muscles tighten. I do, but what if I need it for my run? These gyros can be so sensitive.

"Please," Ajeet begs. "I saw what your robot can do. No way you'll need the spare."

A smile tugs at my lips. He's right: I should be fine. Besides, what's wrong with me? He'd definitely help me if I needed it.

I pop open the lid and check the sectioned-off spaces. "Here," I say when I locate my extra sensor and offer it to him.

His hands are shaking as he takes it from me and dismantles his robot. He pries his failing gyro off the side of the robot's brain-cube and replaces it with mine. For a second, he holds the plug, like he's trying to remember which port to plug it into.

I nudge the black wire with my fingertip. "Port three?"

"Right," he says and plugs the wire into the correct port. "Thanks." He starts to reassemble the rest of his robot.

"Do you have gyro protection?" I ask, stopping him. "It keeps the sensor from jiggling so much."

Ajeet's face is losing color fast. Like he's about to blow chunks. "I shouldn't even be here."

"No, wait," I say, trying to fend off his breakdown—or really his barf-down—as I fish through my crate and hand him a couple of L-brackets.

Ajeet takes the brackets and tries to place them under the new gyro, but his hands keep slipping. He wipes his fingers against his jeans. "I wish my hands weren't so sweaty."

"Here," I say, taking them from him. Feeling his nervous stare, I balance his robot on my lap and place the brackets under the gyro.

"Make sure it's level," he instructs.

I nod and fasten the brackets into place with plastic pegs. When I'm finished, I give it back.

He wipes both hands across his shirt before reassembling the rest of his robot. "Thanks," he says, sounding relieved.

"Is it calibrated to zero?"

Ajeet nods. "I should probably test it, though."

"Ajeet Deshmukh," the judge calls.

"Holy," he croaks.

I hear the *click-click*ing of her heels before I see Mrs. Fuentes rushing up behind us. "It's your turn," she says to him.

"But I need to test it."

"No time." Mrs. Fuentes gestures to the main table. Several eyes stare at us.

My stomach twists. "Don't worry," I say, forcing a smile. "You've got this."

Ajeet nods a little too hard. "I've got this," he says like he's trying to convince himself. He drops his out-of-whack gyro inside his back pocket and repeats the phrase.

Cradling his reassembled robot, he jumps to his feet and hurries over to the main table with Mrs. Fuentes.

When I know he's not looking, my smile falls. I wish we could've tested it first.

I return the cover to my spare-parts crate and set QUEN-10 on top of the lid. With my hands full, I near the table as the judge signals the start of Ajeet's time.

The gym goes quiet—the only sound is the whirring of his robot's oversized wheels. Kids cheer.

His robot moves with precision, on to the second mission. The judge checks off the box for the first completed task. Twenty-five points.

I breathe. Good for him. It's working.

And working. And working.

Ajeet's robot successfully completes mission after mission. The cheers grow louder with each completed task. My face hurts from grinning so much. There are only ten seconds left as he attempts the final mission—the vertical wall climb. His robot's wheels rev and start the climb. I hold my breath, but then his robot tips backward, landing on its side a split second before the final buzzer goes off.

But it doesn't matter. Everyone's screaming and clapping. Mrs. Fuentes is whistling. A kid's arm shoots up and accidentally bumps me. QUEN-10 teeters, but I manage to snatch him before he falls to the ground. "Sorry," the kid says.

Within seconds, Ajeet's score posts: 320. No penalties.

The run was perfect, except for the last task. I'm shouting the loudest. Ajeet spots me on the other side of the table and grins. I give him a thumbs-up as best I can with my hands full. Other kids swarm and pat him on the back.

As they sweep my friend away from the table, my smile fades. Sweat beads on my forehead. His score is going to be tough to beat.

"Rebel Mercer," the judge calls over the noise, inviting me to the starting point at the corner of the table.

I carefully nudge my way through the crowd and place QUEN-10 on home base, setting my spare-parts crate on the floor between my feet.

People are still buzzing about Ajeet's run as the judge announces the start of mine: "Three, two, one." I wipe my forehead and push the center button on QUEN-10.

He rolls across the baseline toward the first task, the one where he should flip the disc and move it into position. "Come on," I say under my breath. He did it this morning. This shouldn't be a problem. The shovel attachment lowers and then stops midair as QUEN-10 edges to the right, ramming into the wall.

His wheels spin with a grinding sound but he's not going anywhere.

I snatch him up, and the judge sets a five-point penalty

disc on the edge of the table, bringing my score to negative five. My fingers tighten around QUEN-10 as I try not to pay attention to the timer, ticking off the seconds. It's okay. Two people move on to Regionals. I can beat Ajeet there.

After I release him the second time, QUEN-10 moves across the baseline and immediately shifts off course, hitting the side again. *Holy!* I snatch him from the edge, taking another grab penalty.

All of a sudden, I think of Dad. He's right: I'm not competitive enough. I can't even win the one thing I'm supposed to be good at.

Think, think. QUEN-10's veering too much. I take a breath, trying to calm down. Did that kid bump him? Did I clutch him too hard when I kept him from falling? I have to fix him. Fast. But how?

Then I remember my spare-parts crate.

I throw off the cover; it smacks against the wooden floor. I spot the space in the bottom right-hand corner, where my spare gyro sensor should be. Empty.

Back on my feet, I search the faces around the table for Ajeet. I need to get my gyro. But where is he? People around me are shaking their heads. Even more aren't paying attention to my miserable run.

Ajeet's right there with them, surrounded by admiring

kids and Mrs. Fuentes, ignoring me. He points something out to her on his robot. I bite the inside of my cheek. *Now* he can talk to her?

"Would you like to try again?" the judge asks.

Only twenty seconds left.

"Ajeet," I call, but he doesn't even look at me. "Ajeet!" He's showing some kid *my* L-brackets under *my* gyro sensor.

My ears go hot. I thought he'd help me if I needed it.

The judge hugs his clipboard to his chest. "Only a few seconds left."

My heart races as I pull QUEN-10 to home base, slamming him into the starting position, willing the impact to fix his gyro. I press start, but now he won't even move. The low battery signal flashes.

"Really?" I shriek as the buzzer goes off. Time's up. My chance is up.

I don't even have to stick around for my score. Negative ten.

So much for showing Dad what a winner I am. Sure, when Aunt Birdie presses him, he might say he loves me anyway. But, deep down, I know he'll never like me. Never.

I grab QUEN-10 and my stuff, storming past Ajeet with his band of admirers. "Thanks a lot for your help," I snap and rush from the gym.

Without stopping to think, I run toward the double glass doors and shove them wide open with my back. I linger on the sidewalk, waiting for Ajeet to catch up. To apologize. To be my best friend.

But he's not following me. Why isn't he following me?

Sweating, I balance my things on my knee and pull the phone from my jeans pocket. No text from him, either.

My crate and robot bobble in my hands as I move, shuffling across the parking lot. The cool morning breeze is gone; the sun bakes the back of my neck. I can't believe I lent Ajeet my spare part. And then I told him how to assemble his robot. And then reinforced it all with my L-brackets.

I kick a rock across the blacktop. What was I thinking? I practically *gave* him his place at Regionals. And how does he pay me back? By ignoring me, that's how.

Before I know it, I'm home. My arms ache from the weight of all the stuff I've been carrying. There's nothing I want more than to throw it inside the house, but Dad's truck is in the driveway. Aunt Birdie's car isn't home yet.

My feet come to an abrupt stop when I spot him, sitting in the driver's seat with the window rolled down. Just my luck. His head is tilted against the headrest, his eyes closed.

If he sees me, it definitely won't be good. Especially after the way things went this morning. Maybe I should go back to school until Aunt Birdie gets home.

"Did you win?" Dad asks, startling me from my escape plan.

My mouth goes dry. My brain rapid-clicks between the only two options: respond or run.

THREE

My arm muscles tremble from the weight of my robotics stuff. I'm so exhausted that if I try to run now, Dad would definitely catch me before I even get to the end of the sidewalk.

A list of possible lies pops into my mind: Mrs. Fuentes canceled the competition; everyone got burrito poisoning; zombies attacked our school—but none of them are remotely believable.

I slowly turn and settle on the truth. "I lost," I admit, bracing for Dad to lay into me about football again. But he sits there, his angular face expressionless, which is even scarier because I can't tell what he's thinking. I clear my throat, ready to change the subject from what a loser I am. "How was the job interview?"

He shakes his head. "Sorry about earlier, bud. I was . . ."

His voice trails off like he doesn't know what else to say.

I stand still, not sure how to react, my arm muscles screaming for relief from the stuff in my hands.

Out of nowhere, Dad slaps the passenger seat, making me jump. I almost drop everything. "Get in," he says as I bobble QUEN-10. "Let's go for a drive."

"That's okay." No way I'm getting in just so he can trap me inside his truck, forcing me to listen to another one of his lectures about how competitive the world is. Forget it.

Dad's expression softens. "Rebs?"

His old nickname catches me off guard. I can't remember the last time he called me that. Definitely before Mom died.

"I think you'll like where we're going."

"Where?" I ask.

He shakes his head with a sly smile. "You'll have to get in to find out."

Even though I'll probably regret it, I'm curious. He doesn't *seem* upset about the competition. I circle the truck and drop QUEN-10 and my parts crate on the floorboard before hopping inside the truck.

We're soon weaving through our neighborhood streets. We don't talk. There's no talk radio, thank goodness. The only sound is the hum of Dad's tires against concrete. I rub my sore arms and shift, growing more uneasy by the second.

What if he changes into Angry Dad again and I'm stuck?

We pass the mall with the best gaming store and head west along the highway until we're outside of town. Dad soon exits, makes a U-turn, and suddenly, I know where we're going.

I smile.

He parks along the side of the road, next to a barbed-wire fence and behind a car with New Mexico plates. On the other side of the fence sits an open pasture with ten cars buried, nose-first, in the ground. Cadillac Ranch.

"This okay?" Dad asks, doubt coloring his voice.

I nod. It's the first time we've been here since right after Mom died. A little over a year ago. She loved this place.

My shoes hit the gravel as Dad retrieves a plastic grocery sack from the bed of his truck. A light breeze moves a strand of hair across my forehead, tickling my face. I sweep it aside before Dad complains about how much I need a haircut again.

We take the dusty path toward the cars. Out here, there's nothing to block our view of where the sky meets the earth, except for a matching set of half-buried Cadillacs.

There are a few tourists, but it's pretty quiet. I point to the cars leaning at the exact same angle. "Did you know these are all slanted at the same angle as the sides of the pyramid at Giza?"

Dad chuckles as we continue along the path. "Actually, I did not know that."

"It's true."

He smiles. "And here I thought it was a field with junky cars."

A couple of kids run in front of us, their feet pounding the hard ground as we reach the Cadillacs. "I'm going to take a look," I say and, when Dad nods, I walk one big circle around them, exploring the colorful graffiti covering each car. Blobs of blue, red, orange, and green. Names and dates in yellow, black, and white. As I pause beside one of the cars, I place my hand on its tire; it spins at my touch.

I think of Ajeet and his big tires. Sudden heat flames my skin. I kick the closest tire, flinching from the pain.

"You look like you could use this," Dad says, tossing a can of silver spray paint. I barely manage to catch it before he takes his can of black paint and pops off the cap, discarding it onto one of the piles of empty cans that litter the ground.

I shake my can, the metal ball rattling inside. Dad pulls his shirt collar over his nose and sprays globular shapes on the underside of one of the Cadillacs. I move over a few cars, and paint my name on the hood. Streaks of liquid silver run down the rainbow colors like glittering rivers across a map.

Mom always called coming here "therapy," a way to release the bad feelings trapped inside. My shoulders relax with each tap on the nozzle as I think of her. She always knew how to help me. Too bad she couldn't do the same for Dad, especially after he came home with PTSD.

Mom's the one who came up with the term "Angry Dad." It was our secret code name when he got bad, the times Dad couldn't seem to think of anything but the horrible things he'd heard and seen. *It's Angry Dad: Let's go for a walk,* she'd say. *It's Angry Dad again: Let's go camping to give him the space he needs.*

To my right, I spy Dad spray-paint a black sun and moon— that militia symbol again. My neck tightens. I looked it up on the internet: the sun and moon means the Flag Bearers are watching both day and night.

Dad pulls his shirt from his nose. "They hired a Mexican," he says, his voice gruff.

I glance sideways at another family as they move past us, hoping they didn't hear.

"They didn't even give me a chance," he adds.

My sprayer keeps spraying, even though I'm not really paying attention to my silver marks.

"Didn't matter I'd served our country for the last seventeen years."

"That's ridiculous," I say, and I mean it. Why wouldn't someone hire my dad after all he's done to protect our country's freedoms? He deserves a good job as much as anyone else. More, even.

"They said he'd work for less money than me, so they hired him instead. I guess they want subpar work." Dad tosses his used can into the pile with a *clang*.

My fingers tighten around the paint in my hand as I keep spraying.

"Did that kid win today?" Dad asks, wiping his forehead with his sleeve.

My finger comes off the sprayer. By *that kid*, I know he means Ajeet. I nod.

"Jeez, I told you. The government is letting them in by the droves." He wags his finger at me. "You know they're trying to shut us out, don't you?"

I don't know how to respond.

His hand drops with a sigh. "Sometimes, I think it'd be better if we could get away from here." He stares into the distance. "Go someplace quiet."

"Like where?" I whisper, so I don't startle him.

He doesn't take his eyes off the horizon; he doesn't answer.

In the awkward silence, I pull my phone from my pocket to give me something to stare at, too. With the paint can in one hand, I tap my screen with the other. There's a text from Ajeet from a few minutes ago: *Where are you? The award ceremony is about to start.*

Fire flashes through my insides. I hurriedly close the text without answering.

"I bet he pretended to be your friend," Dad says.

The way he says it makes me look up. "Who?"

"That kid with the robot."

"I *thought* he was my friend," I admit, shoving my phone inside my pocket. But Ajeet didn't help me, even though I helped him.

"It's always the same," Dad replies. "It's happened to me at least a dozen times. They steal what belongs to us. He probably gained your trust first, right?"

I wince, dropping the paint can in the dirt. *Did* Ajeet pretend he was my friend so I'd help him? My cheeks flush with a mix of anger and shame as I think of him bragging to Mrs. Fuentes when I needed his help. "I helped him win today."

Dad's jaw tightens. "See there?"

It feels good to have Dad on my side for a change.

"He didn't even know what port to put the gyro into," I

add, though it's not completely true. Ajeet knew: He was just nervous.

Dad shakes his head. "Typical. They use you until they get promoted and then leave you in the dust without even looking back."

Another text comes through but I ignore it. "Exactly."

Dad's nodding. He's angry, but not at me. He's angry *for* me. *With* me. "Did he offer to help you when you needed it?"

"No," I grumble. "He was too busy celebrating."

Dad pounds a fist against the buried car, and it feels good. Almost as good as if I'd done it myself.

"Rebel, nothing is going to change until we're willing to do something about it." His expression is tired, but fierce.

I like how he's included me. "What can I do?"

"It's time we take a stand."

FOUR

Time for me to take a stand.

Dad is right. We've both been cheated today. He deserved that job—he *needed* that job—and it was stolen from him. I deserved to win, and it was stolen from me. Ajeet used me.

By the time we get home, I'm fuming. It feels like my fingers and toes are on fire.

I know exactly what I have to do.

Aunt Birdie still isn't here—thank goodness—because she's got some kind of internal radar that goes off when she suspects I'm up to something.

I jump out onto the driveway, leaving QUEN-10, and hurry to the rear of Dad's truck. I reach over the side of the truck bed and rifle through the plastic grocery sack, cans clinking against one another, until I find what I need. "Can I borrow this?" I ask, holding a can of red spray paint.

Dad's already at the front door of our house. I move around to the other side of the truck so he can see what I'm holding. His eyes narrow.

"It's—for a science project," I lie. "Due tomorrow." Aunt Birdie says most liars won't look you in the eyes. I lock my knees and force myself not to look away.

Dad nods and opens the door. I hang by his truck, trying to come up with my next excuse of why I need to go back to school. He turns in the threshold before I can think. "Is there something else?"

"Uh." Lying is a lot harder than it looks. Especially when your very large, very intimidating Marine dad is staring at you. I bite my lip when, out of nowhere, it comes to me.

My laugh comes out shallow. "I guess I was in such a hurry that I left my backpack at school." *True.* I clear my throat, inching down the driveway. "And I need it for my project." *Not true.*

Dad rubs his eyes and swings his key ring around his index finger, making the keys jingle. "I wish you'd said something before we got home, Rebs." He starts to close the door to the house.

"That's okay," I say, a little too loud, stopping him. I let out another dumb laugh and then lower my voice. "Go ahead and take a nap. I don't mind walking." My feet hit the sidewalk, and I take off. The metal ball rattles inside the paint can as my arm swings back and forth.

I check over my shoulder; he's not chasing me. I'm practically running to school. If they stop me when I get there, I'll tell them I forgot my backpack in my locker. Hopefully, they don't ask me about the paint in my hand.

There are still a few cars in the lot. The vans are gone.

I pass through the glass doors and look to my left. The light's still on inside the gym. I hear voices, and then laughter. Specifically, Ajeet's snorty laugh. My hand tightens around the paint can.

Hot anger spreads like venom throughout my body. With the paint can clenched in my hand, I hurry along the empty hallway, my shoes pounding against the polished floors.

I make a right and then a left until I'm in the seventh-grade hallway. Lockers line the walls. Fluorescents buzz overhead, but all of the classrooms are dark.

The changing light from the overhead TV monitor catches my eye. The slides on the screen alternate, announcing upcoming games, pep rallies, and the science fair. Next, a picture flashes onto the screen: My *EX*-best friend is grinning. He's holding his robot and pointing to my L-brackets beneath my gyro sensor. And then a message scrolls across the screen: *Congratulations to our robotics champion, Ajeet Deshmukh!*

I can't believe it. He won.

Before I can think, I pop the lid off the paint can and release red lines and curves against the gray metal doors. Every bit of me is on fire as I spray large letters, stretching them across the entire wall of lockers. My chest heaves with each breath. I make the final dot on the exclamation point. Red paint dribbles to the floor.

Satisfied, I back away from my work. I'm panting like I do when the PE coaches make us run laps.

I read my message. Then I hear a gasp—mine.

All of a sudden, it feels like I've been plunged into a pool of ice. The can drops from my hand with a loud *clang*. The can jangles as it rolls across the floor and stops when it hits the opposite wall.

Chills run along my arms as I read the message again. What have I done?

My breath stutters as I search the hall for something to clean it off.

Nothing.

What have I done?

I take the bottom of my T-shirt and wipe the exclamation

point, but it only smears the paint. My gaze darts and then lands on the door to the boys' restroom. Paper towels and water. That should get it off, right?

The *click-click*ing of heels, alongside the *squeak* of tennis shoes, suddenly echoes from the next hallway.

My heart jumps to my throat. No! What have I done?

There are voices I don't recognize and a couple I do: Mrs. Fuentes and . . . Ajeet.

I want to scream. I will myself to move, but guilt keeps me frozen, trapped like I'm in a block of ice.

Mrs. Fuentes rounds the corner; the smile immediately falls from her lips. Her eyes fill with disbelief and then disappointment. Within seconds, she shuffles in front of Ajeet, trying to block his view. But he edges around her.

A gray-bearded man I don't recognize stands, wide-eyed, between Ajeet and the girl from the competition, the one in the unicorn T-shirt. "What a jerk," she mutters, like a slap to my face. She turns to Ajeet. "I thought you said he was your friend." Like a punch to my gut.

I can't look at him. What have I done? While I was painting hate across a wall of lockers, he told this girl we were friends.

"Rebel?" Ajeet says, his voice wavy.

My stomach clenches at the sound. I instantly regret looking at him. I absorb the hurt in his eyes. *I'm so sorry,* I want to say. *I don't really mean it.*

But the red words I've painted scream louder: GO BACK TO WHERE YOU CAME FROM, AJEET!

My friend turns away, and the last thing I see is him wiping his tears before he vanishes.

My lower lip trembles.

"Mr. Mercer," Mrs. Fuentes snaps, startling me. Her face pinches. Her usual smile is gone. "My office." She turns to the girl and the man, her voice softer. "I'm so sorry. Will you please excuse me?" Then she faces me with a scowl.

I look down in shame. There's red paint on my hands. On my T-shirt. My jeans. It looks like I'm bleeding to death. It feels like I am.

"*Now,* Mr. Mercer." Mrs. Fuentes snags me by the elbow with a rough hand. My feet come unstuck as she drags me along the hall making me stumble.

"See you at Regionals," the man calls behind us, and I realize he's the girl's teacher, and she's the one who's going to Regionals instead of me.

How did everything get so messed up?

When we reach her office, Mrs. Fuentes releases my arm.

"Sit," she orders, and I drop into one of the straight-backed, wooden chairs in front of her desk. "Don't move." She storms away, slamming the door behind her.

I don't dare look over my shoulder, but I can hear her make the call. The clock on the wall shows it's already after five. Aunt Birdie is probably home by now. I think of my red message again and shift in the chair, guilt wrapping around me like a tight blanket. What will my aunt think of me? Will she look totally disappointed like Mrs. Fuentes?

My gaze nervously jumps from the porcelain cats on my principal's shelf to the stack of papers haphazardly thrown into a wire basket. Silver-framed pictures of Mrs. Fuentes's husband and son sit on the credenza beneath the window. There's one of her son in front of the NASA sign.

My heart sinks. My chances of living long enough to become an engineer are pretty much zero.

Through the slats in the blinds, I spot Aunt Birdie hurrying toward the building. For a second, I'm relieved it's not Dad. But then I spy her worried face as she fidgets with her purse strap, trying to get it over her shoulder, before she slips out of sight.

Within seconds, I hear her. "Is he okay?" she asks.

Strange to ask if I'm okay. Mrs. Fuentes must not have told her what I've done.

"Please step inside," my principal says. The door opens, and her rose perfume fills my nose.

"What happened?" Aunt Birdie asks as Mrs. Fuentes settles into the swivel chair behind her desk.

My knees bob as I wait for her to announce my crime. But she shakes her head and points to my aunt.

She wants *me* to tell her? "Um," I say, but my voice comes out weird. I rub my paint-stained hands across my jeans.

Aunt Birdie sits in the chair next to me. Her Star Wars scrubs shift, exposing her mismatched socks. She sighs. "I already know what you did."

My gaze moves away from her socks. "You do?" I ask, focusing on the silver cross around her neck, afraid to see the disappointment in her eyes.

"Rebel," she says. Her face matches her voice: soft, not angry. Her blue eyes examine me, like she's trying to understand this stranger sitting next to her. "Why, honey?" she asks.

"I don't know," I answer because it's the easiest thing to say when there's not an easy answer. The reasons keep sliding around and changing places in my brain, like the colored squares on a Rubik's Cube. I was confused. Dad didn't get the job he deserved. I was angry. He was hurt. I was, too. I was angry. Ajeet took my parts. I wanted to win. I lost the competition. I was embarrassed. I thought Ajeet used me. I was angry. He didn't come after me. I was hurt.

"You can talk to me," Aunt Birdie says, her voice nudging but still soothing. It's probably one of the things that makes her such a great nurse. She taps my stained hand. "I can tell you're thinking over there."

"What *were* you thinking?" Mrs. Fuentes says, her voice tight. "You have never done anything like this before."

I shrug, and Mrs. Fuentes leans back in her chair, her mouth forming a narrow line.

Aunt Birdie takes one of my hands. Normally, I'd pull away. But it actually feels nice she still wants to. She squeezes. "You are not this person, Rebel. Did your dad put you up to this?"

I chew my bottom lip. Did Dad put me up to this? I shake my head. No, not really.

"Then, *what* happened?"

I wish I could tell her: *I want Dad to be proud of me. I get so angry sometimes. I don't like some of the things he says. But I still want him to like me for who I am.* I open my mouth to try.

Out of nowhere, heavy footsteps interrupt as Dad barges into my principal's office. I yank my hand from Aunt Birdie's.

She shakes her head. "Nathan, I told you I'd take care of this."

My fingers clutch the sides of my seat.

"He's *my* son," Dad says, slapping his chest.

I want to slip under Mrs. Fuentes's desk and hide.

His glare shifts to my principal. "If you're done here—"

"We absolutely are *not* done." Mrs. Fuentes rises from her chair. "Your son has defaced school property, not to mention the fact he's used hate speech to do it."

I cringe; Dad scoffs.

"Nathan, please," Aunt Birdie says, rising from her chair.

They're hovering over me. I *really* don't want to be here.

Mrs. Fuentes presses her index finger against the desk. "We have a zero tolerance policy at this school for vandalism, especially when it includes hate speech."

Dad folds his arms over his chest. "Is that what you're calling the truth these days?"

I slump further in my chair.

My principal furrows her brow and looks to Aunt Birdie. "Miss Mercer, I'm sorry, but I have no choice but to expel Rebel."

"What?" I ask, my voice cracking.

"Mrs. Fuentes, please," my aunt says. "I think there's a reason here and—"

"You don't need to defend him to *her*," Dad says, jabbing his finger in the air. "She's clearly one of them. Look at her."

Mrs. Fuentes's hands curl into fists. Aunt Birdie's face goes bright red. My heart races.

"Come on, Rebel," Dad says. "We're leaving."

Without thinking, I jump to attention, following his order. As I leave the office, I can hear my aunt apologizing.

"My decision's final," Mrs. Fuentes says, her tone sharp.

I wince as I follow Dad. I've royally screwed up. I've disappointed my aunt, and now she's going to worry about me, too. I've managed to lose the competition, my school, and, worst of all, my best friend.

In a span of a few hours, I've lost everything.

FIVE

"You don't need to put up with that garbage," Dad says as he marches toward his truck in the school parking lot.

It's filled with suitcases and boxes. Crates crammed with my comic books and robotics stuff are in the bed of his truck. "Where?" I ask, unsteady. "Where are we going?"

The school door slams shut behind us. "I can't believe you!" Aunt Birdie shouts.

"What?" Dad asks.

"Don't give me that," she says. "You know exactly what I'm talking about."

He waves his hand at the school. "That woman's clearly biased."

Aunt Birdie shoots him a pointed look. "And you clearly haven't started therapy like you said you would."

I hold my breath, picking at the dried red paint on my thumbnail.

Dad flings open the passenger-side door on his truck and unlocks the glove compartment, snatching a piece of paper from inside. "Here," he says, shoving the crumpled page in her hand.

"What's this?" Aunt Birdie smooths the letter against her pant leg. There's a government seal at the top.

He twists the ring on his left hand. "My disability rating was too low," Dad says, his voice quieter. Like all the fight has left him. "My doctors don't agree on my PTSD."

I exhale. It's the first time I've heard Dad say it out loud: He has PTSD.

Aunt Birdie holds up the letter. "I'm sure we can appeal."

Dad shakes his head. "Look, I just want to get away for a while. Get out of the city. I think being out in nature where it's peaceful will help clear my head." He rubs a hand across his cheek. "I'd also like to spend some time with Rebel."

Is he serious?

He sighs. "Ever since Jenny died, there really hasn't been much of a chance for us to do stuff together, with me being gone and everything."

I shift, surprised to hear him mention Mom.

"I don't know," Aunt Birdie says.

"I've missed so much already."

Does he really want to spend time with *me*?

Dad nods, as if he can hear what I'm thinking. He steps closer, becoming the top point of our family's acute triangle. "We could go fishing. Hiking. Maybe even ride some four-wheelers if you want?" It's a question, not an order.

"And where would you go?" Aunt Birdie asks, sounding skeptical. "We have to figure out his school situation."

"There's the campground in Sipapu," Dad says as he points northwest. "I thought it'd be fun for him to go since it was so special to his—"

"Mom," I whisper to myself.

Dad nods with a smile.

Sometimes, Mom and I would go camping there when Dad was home on military leave—the times Mom would explain the reason only the two of us were going as: *Angry Dad needs to stay home and work on his demons.*

Aunt Birdie clutches her purse strap. "I don't think running away is the right lesson here."

"I really need this, Bird," Dad says before turning to me. "What do you think? Would you like to come?"

What do I think? I think my life has spun out of control like QUEN-10.

Aunt Birdie touches my arm. "You don't have to go. You're welcome to stay right here with me."

"And do what?" Dad asks. "The boy got expelled."

I cringe, but he's right. I've messed up everything.

Aunt Birdie wrings her hands. "I'm sure if you both go inside and apologize—"

"I thought you wanted me to get better," Dad interrupts.

Her hands stop. "That's unfair, and you know it."

I can feel the tension rising between them again. Mrs. Fuentes is probably looking through her blinds, gathering even more evidence for why I should be expelled.

"It's okay," I say, hoping to extinguish the fight before it restarts. "I want to go."

"You do?" My aunt doesn't even try to hide the shock on her face.

Dad immediately puts his arm around me; I can smell his pine aftershave. I can't remember the last time he wanted to be anywhere this close to me.

Aunt Birdie shakes her head. "What about school?"

"He's *my* son," Dad says, squeezing my shoulder, almost too tight. "I haven't forgotten. Have you?"

Aunt Birdie's lip quivers, making me question my decision.

He loosens his grip. "You've been wonderful, sis." Dad rounds the front of his truck. "But we need this. *I* need this.

And we'll get his schooling figured out soon enough."

When he's behind the wheel, my aunt edges closer and whispers, "You don't have to do this."

"I know," I say. "I want to." At least, part of me wants to go. There's nothing left for me here. Besides, Dad may not give me another chance.

Without warning, Aunt Birdie hugs me so hard I think she's going to snap my spine. Even *she's* stronger than I am.

"Call me with your cell if you need anything," she says. "Anything at all." She releases me.

"I'll be fine," I say, tapping the phone in my pocket. I hate that she worries so much.

Before she has a chance to sense my doubt, I hop into the truck and shut the door. Dad slides two bug-out bags over and carefully places them in the back seat.

The engine roars to life. "We're going to get our life back, Rebs." Dad points to a piece of paper on the console between us—a letter that was covered by the bags until now.

But this letter doesn't have a government seal at the top. It has the black sun and moon of the Flag Bearers.

A lump forms in my throat as I quickly read the invitation for my dad to train with the militia in Oklahoma.

"What do you think?" he asks, his voice hopeful. "I know it's not New Mexico, but I was hoping you'd still want to come with me." He almost looks shy in asking. "We could still go fishing and hiking. I hear it's really pretty there this time of year."

Normally, I would think this was a bad idea. *Way* bad. Why would he tell Aunt Birdie we're going to New Mexico when we're really going to Oklahoma?

Of course, if there's one thing I've figured out about Dad, it's that I haven't figured him out. Not even close. Maybe this trip can change that.

"Rebs?" Dad asks, his voice soft.

I've already managed to mess up my whole life in a single afternoon. Have I really got anything to lose? Besides, he's not ordering me to go. He's asking me.

And maybe if we're away from all the normal life stress, he'll get better. Maybe I won't feel so angry all the time. And what if I can help him? Wouldn't it be wrong to say no?

I clear my throat and nod. "Let's go."

SIX

A loud slam jolts me awake; I exhale a ring of fog onto the passenger-side window and rub my eyes. Through the clouded glass, I spot Dad sliding on his black jacket as he walks away from the truck into a convenience store. The parking lot and other pumps are empty. There's a red-and-white sign on the front of the building: DAIRY MART & GAS.

I sit up. Where are we?

The last thing I remember is getting drowsy somewhere between the drive-through at the burger place in Middle-of-Nowhere, Oklahoma, and the turnoff of I-40. I run my tongue along my teeth and taste our greasy dinner all over again.

The smell of stale french fries and gasoline hovers in the air. My neck cracks as I turn my head and hear the glugging sound of fuel filling our tank. The clock on the truck's dash reads almost three in the morning. The lights around me glow bright, like the ones on an alien ship, but the rest of the world is dark.

I unbuckle my seat belt and stretch when, from out of nowhere, a pair of headlights pierces the distant darkness. My arms drop as the orange truck speeds through a flashing traffic light. The truck's tires screech, spinning and moving closer, until it comes to a stop. Right next to me.

A man with a tan baseball cap and reddish-brown mustache turns off his engine before snatching his assault rifle from the seat. My heart skips a beat; I immediately lock the door. Like that will keep him from shooting me.

But he's not even looking at me. Not yet anyway. He nears the store.

I suddenly remember Dad and angle my neck so I can get a better view. Through the convenience store window, I spot him. Dad's head is bent as he gets coffee from a machine. The man with the gun is almost to the door.

He's going to rob the store. And my dad's inside.

With one eye on the robber, I lean against the window, trying to get his license plate so I can memorize the number, but it's no use. It's covered in mud.

Think, think.

Suddenly, the man spins, revealing a wide scar running

along his neck and up the side of his face. His eyes narrow when he spots me staring at him.

I drop to the floorboard, tucking myself beneath the glove compartment, and pull my phone from my pocket. My hand shakes as I swipe the screen.

No service. *No!*

What am I going to do?

From my hiding spot on the floor, my ears strain, listening for gunshots. But I only hear the low murmur of voices, followed by approaching footsteps. I curl my long legs against my chest, trying to make myself as small as possible, desperate to figure out a way to save Dad.

Someone flips the door handle. My pulse races. *Don't shoot. Please. Don't shoot.* I draw my knees under my chin and spot Dad's handgun, hidden under the driver's seat.

Should I grab it? The thought makes my stomach clench.

There's another *click* of a lock; I squeeze my eyelids shut and hear the door swing open. Cold air rushes in; goose bumps rise along my arms.

"Rebel?" Dad says.

My eyes fly open. He's looking at me like he doesn't recognize me. Like I'm a mutant porg instead of his son.

"Get in," I say, frantic. "We have to get out of here!"

The man with the wide, pinkish scar leans inside our

truck. My feet push against the floor mat, but there's nowhere to go. He grasps the base of his gun. The skin on his hand is shiny, matching the side of his face and neck. Like the whole right side of his body has been burned.

I swallow hard. Why is Dad just standing there?

The man shakes his head. "*This* is the boy you've been describing?"

Under the bright lights, Dad's face tightens. "Get up," he barks.

Confusion clutters my mind.

As they ease away from the door, I nervously follow Dad's order, sliding from the truck before landing between them. My numb legs fold beneath my weight. Dad yanks my T-shirt to prevent me from eating pavement. He doesn't spill a drop of his coffee.

The man rubs a scarred hand across his chin as he looks down on me. "Not exactly what I'd pictured." There's a black sun and moon on the front of his cap.

My cheeks flush with embarrassment as Dad releases me. I grasp the edge of the door, my legs tingling as they slowly regain feeling.

Dad clears his throat. "Rebel, this is Wade Kissop, our militia leader."

The gun. It suddenly all makes sense. He's not a robber.

He's the guy who invited us here. Wherever *here* is.

Wade sneers as he slides the rifle from his shoulder and rests the bottom of it on the ground. "You two done playing hide-and-seek, or should I wait until you hand out the lollipops?"

I wince.

"Let's go," Wade says.

Dad's heels slide together, his spine straight, arms to his side. "Yes, sir."

It surprises me how fast he snaps into Marine mode. Still not a drop of coffee spilled.

But Wade doesn't even acknowledge my dad standing at attention. Doesn't he know he's an American hero? I clench my jaw as Wade hops into his truck instead and rolls down the window. He jerks his thumb toward the darkness. "Follow me up the mountain."

My gaze follows the direction he's pointing. What mountain? I don't see any mountain.

"Yes, sir," Dad repeats.

Wade's engine rumbles as he edges away. Smoke curls from the tailpipe.

"Get in," Dad orders.

In no time, we're speeding along a two-lane highway. Wade's in front of us, driving like a maniac. Dad presses the accelerator; the needle on the speedometer climbs over eighty miles per hour. We zip past the occasional shack in a blur, but there's mostly blackness. It's so dark; it seems like the lights on our trucks are the only ones on the whole planet. Maybe the entire universe.

As my eyes adjust, the grays and blacks around us become more defined. Straight ahead, I spot the black outline of a mountain, set against a starry sky. There are billions of stars surrounding us. It's like we can see the whole galaxy out here. I wonder if they can see us.

"Did you really have to embarrass me like that?"

My shoulders sink.

Dad lowers his empty coffee cup into the cup holder and jabs his finger at the floor of the truck, where I'd been hiding. "What were you even doing down there?"

I rub the last of the sleep from my eyes. Angry Dad is back.

"I asked you a question."

Oh, not much. Just hiding from your new friend with the assault rifle. I shift in my seat. "I—"

"Never mind," he snaps, cutting me off. He gases the engine; the truck begins to climb. "I don't want to know."

I bite my bottom lip and turn away. The trees thicken the higher we head up the mountain. Maybe Aunt Birdie was right: Maybe I should've stayed in Amarillo.

My ears fill with the sudden change in pressure as we take the switchbacks up the mountain. We're probably about two-thirds up when a dull glow appears through the trees to my right. It must be the town below. If I squint, I can almost pick out the Dairy Mart & Gas.

We make another turn, and the town is gone. The rest of the world is gone. I hold my breath.

Dad slows only slightly before our tires squeal, peeling off the paved road. We bounce in a rut, forcing me to exhale. Someone has cut a dirt road just wide enough for a truck to fit between the trees. Dad is going so fast we jolt and dip against the uneven ground. Ahead of us, Wade's taillights bounce erratically. My teeth chatter from the force.

I will myself not to scream as we almost crash into a tree. Dad shifts into four-wheel drive, his face tight with concentration. The engine groans from the strain.

My fingers reach and wrap around the grab bar. I clench my jaw shut so I don't crack a tooth. A branch scrapes the side of the truck, and I'm thankful we ate hours ago or I'd definitely be covered in puke.

After several minutes of bumping and swaying and dropping, we finally reach a clearing with a line of parked trucks. Dad swerves in next to them and kills the engine. He's not even breathing hard.

I'm a mess—sweating, panting, shaky hands.

Dad jumps from the driver's seat. Leaves crunch where he lands. He grabs our bug-out bags and slams the door closed.

"I'm fine," I grumble to the empty truck. "In case you were wondering."

I open the door and hop to the ground. The sudden chill in the air makes me shiver. I grab my gray hoodie with the *Man Vs Robot* silhouettes on the chest.

Without waiting for me, Wade and Dad march uphill, disappearing between the trees.

Heat flushes my fingers. Oh sure, no problem. Don't wait for me. It's only the middle of the night, and I really wanted to go on a nature hike. Thanks for asking.

I pull out my phone to text Aunt Birdie to let her know we made it (barely). But there's still no service. I wave my phone around—like that will help—but it's no use. I nearly throw it against a tree, but then make myself stop. I force a deep breath and shove it inside my jeans pocket instead. I'll text her when we get to wherever it is we're going.

My shoes brush through the leaves as I climb. The smell of decay rises as I hurry to catch up. But I'm already winded from the altitude.

My lungs burn. I bend over, breathing hard, my hands

on my knees. Who am I kidding? It's not the altitude: I'm totally out of shape.

And I've lost them. We've been here less than five minutes, and I've already lost them. My heart thuds as I try to catch my breath. Dad's going to be so mad.

From out of nowhere, a brisk shadow slips between the trees. My breath catches. I look harder but don't see anything. Was it a bear? Do they even have bears in Oklahoma? I don't stick around long enough to find out.

I pick up the pace, willing myself to keep moving uphill in the general direction I think they're headed. Eventually, I hear the low grumble of voices and cut toward the sound.

The moment I exit the trees and move into another clearing, a light shines straight into my eyes, blinding me. I come to an abrupt halt, almost falling and tripping on my own feet.

"Where do you think you're going?" a harsh voice asks.

I put up my hands and could swear my fingers brush against the tip of a gun.

SEVEN

My fingers jerk back from the gun as I try to shield my eyes with one hand, but it's no use. I can't see a thing.

"It's okay," someone says from off to my right. "The boy's with us."

All of a sudden, the flashlight clicks off; I see a million stars. But these aren't in the sky.

"That's my son," Dad says, and I'm both surprised and relieved he's claimed me.

There's movement in front of me. "Name's Dwight."

"Rebel," I say weakly. The stars slowly fade when I see the tall, hairy guy—hairy arms, hairy head, hairy hairs sticking out from the top of his black shirt. He drops the flashlight in a loop on his belt. With all the brown hair and his overbite, Dwight reminds me of Chewbacca, except this guy carries an assault rifle.

I take a step backward.

Several feet in front of me I can make out the outline of a long building with yellow lights glowing on the corners. Moths flit around the dim bulbs. It almost feels like a dream with everything hazy along the edges.

Then my gaze fixes on the words painted on the gray siding: FLAG BEARERS ✺ WHITES ONLY. Not a dream. Make that a nightmare. I don't know what I was expecting, but it wasn't this.

I take another step backward, wondering if I'll be able to find the truck if I make a run for it. Will they shoot me if I try?

"Boy's not exactly how you described him, is he?" The scar along Wade's jawline tightens as he gestures at the *Man Vs Robot* on my hoodie.

I fold my arms over my chest, hiding the logo.

"Seems scared of his own shadow."

There's a *snap* as a massive light comes on at my back. A shadow appears on the ground before me, making me jump and proving I am, in fact, scared of my own shadow.

There's a tall watchtower behind me. The lantern at the top swivels on a stand, sweeping the camp with a wide beam of light. A few cabins sit scattered throughout the woods. Off to the far right, there's some kind of maze and a firing range with human-shaped targets. Closer in sits the large building with the racist sign.

The man behind the lantern glowers at me. I promptly look away.

"What's he searching for?" Dad asks, pointing to the man in the watchtower.

Wade spits in the dirt. "New World Order scum."

I open my mouth to ask what that is, but Dad throws me a sharp look. I press my lips closed.

Wade points to the dark sky. "He spotted a helicopter flying over camp the other day."

"Unmarked?" Dad asks.

"Of course," Wade says. "Flat black paint."

"New World Order," they both conclude before Wade looks to the tower. "See anything, Karl?"

The man in the tower shakes his head. "All clear, sir."

"Good, then come on down so I can introduce you to our new recruit."

The lantern immediately goes dark. It pops as it cools. In less than thirty seconds, Karl is on the ground, standing in front of me. He's got an assault weapon, too. They all have guns. Karl is about the same age as Dad, but even more muscular with light, light blond hair. The only thing he's missing is the Nazi uniform they wear in those old war movies.

Instead, the three of them are wearing camo pants with long-sleeved black T-shirts, black boots, and an automatic weapon. I shiver. Why did I think this was a good idea again?

Karl smirks like he can see right through me. "What the hell's this kid doing here?" His icy blue eyes stay locked on me like I'm some kind of prey.

"He's with me," Dad says.

Karl's mouth twists in disgust. "Is that right?" He turns to Wade. "This kid clearly doesn't belong here. Look at him."

I flinch.

"He could get hurt, or worse, injure someone in the unit."

Dad surges toward him. "Who are you to dictate who can and can't stay?"

"Dad," I say, not knowing what else to do.

Karl shoves him backward. "You're out of line, soldier."

The muscles in Dad's neck tighten.

Dwight rubs his hairy hands together, like he's ready for the first round bell to sound.

"Alright, gentlemen," Wade says as he moves between them. A cruel smile stretches the scar against his cheekbone. "Nathan, meet Karl Thompson, head of security."

Karl lifts his chin.

Dad's fists loosen.

"I'm sure Karl will come around," Wade says to Dad and

then gestures to me. "Once he sees your boy shoot."

Sees me *what*?

"You did say Rebel was an excellent marksman, right?"

My mouth falls slack. He said *what*?

Karl looks at Dad likes he doesn't believe a word of it now that he's seen me. Which is totally legitimate.

"Of course," Dad says, extending his hand to Karl. "Shake?" It seems like a friendly gesture, but it feels like a bull stomping his foot before he attacks.

Karl takes Dad's hand and they shake, veins popping in their necks. I can practically smell the testosterone pulsing between them.

I cross my arm over my chest and squeeze my skinny bicep.

Karl releases Dad's hand. "Karl Thompson, gunnery sergeant."

My shoulders stiffen another notch. He's a whole rank above Dad.

"Karl was in the Marines like you," Wade adds.

"Nathan Mercer, *former* staff sergeant."

Dwight smacks his lips, like he can taste the fight rekindling. I almost expect him to let out an excited Chewbacca gurgle.

Karl scoffs. "With what the New World Order's been up

to lately, I think we're *all* former U.S. military here, don't you?"

"Not me," Dwight says. "I was a cop over in Chisom County."

Karl's face relaxes a bit. "And you won't ever let us forget it, either."

Wade slaps Dad on the shoulder with his scarred hand; Dad winces. "You must be exhausted. What do you say we get some shut-eye and exchange war stories in the morning?"

I shake my head. That's the last thing Dad needs to do.

"I've already had the boys unload and bring your things to the cabin. I hope you don't mind."

"Thank you, sir," Dad says.

"Karl will show you there now." Wade glances over at me, his eyes narrowing. "See you soldiers in the morning."

I swallow hard. This guy definitely wants to kill me.

Wade slowly turns away and, with Dwight as his hairy shadow, they disappear into the trees.

"Follow me," Karl says, clicking on his flashlight. He marches the opposite direction and begins the uphill climb.

Dad grabs the bug-out bags before he nears, handing one to me with a whisper. "I think this is going to work. You?"

I take the heavy bag; my arms drop from the weight.

"Y-yes, sir," I say to his eager face. I don't have the heart to tell him these guys are total lunatics.

As he turns to follow Karl, I promise myself I'll try harder not to embarrass him again. I heave the backpack over my shoulders, holding my groan inside my mouth, and bend from the bag's weight as I walk.

The beam on Karl's flashlight sweeps across the bark of the surrounding trees. Tiny leaves brush against my arms and face.

Focused on trying to keep up with Karl's moving light ahead, I trip over a branch and drop, smacking my knee against a sharp rock.

I gasp from the sting and bite the inside of my cheek, falling backward like a turtle on its shell. I draw my leg against my chest. The rock sliced my jeans. Of course it did. My knee is bleeding. It's definitely going to leave a bruise.

Leaves rustle with footsteps. I tense against the cold ground, praying it's not Karl.

"You alright?" Dad asks as he approaches. I exhale as he crouches next to me. So much for not embarrassing him.

I nod, forcing myself to be tough. I roll onto my side and then manage to sit, propping the bug-out bag against the branch I tripped over, trying to leverage the bag's weight. "Yes, sir," I say, hoping I sound stronger than I feel.

"Take my hand," he says, and I do. He easily uproots me from the ground. "Karl says it's only a little farther."

When he releases me, I slump forward from the bag's weight. My knee aches, but I don't dare let on. "I can make it," I assure him, ignoring the throbbing in my knee, the sore muscles in my back.

We continue uphill through the trees. The rushing sound of water grows louder with each step until we reach Karl. He's standing on the edge of a creek, waiting for us.

I close my mouth to keep from panting.

"Where now?" Dad asks, not even winded.

Karl levels his beam on a flat rock about the diameter of a dinner plate in the center of the creek. "Watch your step," he says.

"What are we doing?" I ask. Because I know they don't expect me to leap across this river, especially not with this bag on my back. Not when I'm the one who always eats sand when I'm forced to do the long jump at school.

"You can do it," Dad says and hops across easily. Of course he does. His dark silhouette watches from the other side of the creek.

Karl instantly turns to me and points the flashlight into the woods behind us. Away from us.

I think he's about to push me like my PE coach does.

"Does your mom know you're here?" he says under the sound of the running creek.

"My mom?" I ask, surprised. No one's asked me about her for at least six months. I shift uneasily, feeling Dad's stare from the other side.

"What's going on?" Dad shouts.

Karl leans in, and I can feel his hot breath on my face. "You don't belong here." He touches his gun. "You're not *safe.*"

My legs give a little. What does he mean *I'm not safe*? The darkness masks Karl's face; I can't tell whether it's a warning or a threat. I don't want to find out.

I spin toward the water and leap.

EIGHT

My foot actually makes contact with the rock in the center of the creek. And then, it slips. The weight of the backpack pulls me sideways. I overcompensate, jerking the opposite direction, trying to right myself, but it's too late. I fall into the water with a splash.

I gasp from the cold shock. The creek engulfs my arms, my legs. I gulp a mouthful of silty water. My muscles seize; bubbles rush against my eardrums. My arms flap wildly, palms smacking the surface until a hand snatches my wrist.

Water pushes against my chest. The creek is trying to whisk me downstream. There's a muffled voice. The hand tightens around my wrist and yanks, straining my shoulder. My face surfaces for a second. Karl shouts from the rock, holding on to me, but my mind doesn't compute what he's saying.

My face plunges beneath the surface and then bobs up.

"Rebel!" Dad yells from the bank. "Stand up!"

Stand?

With Karl squeezing my wrist, I work to swing my legs against the current, pushing my feet until they find the rocks at the bottom.

Water rushes from my body as I stand. I hack and cough, trying to clear water and dirt from my lungs. With my free hand, I swipe the dripping hair from my eyes and spy Dad staring at me from the bank. It's too dark to see his expression, but I can already feel his disappointment.

The rushing creek only comes to my waist. If I weren't so cold, I know I'd be feeling the warmth of shame across my cheeks. While I was flailing like a helpless moron, I could have stood this whole time.

No wonder Dad lies about me.

"Can you make it to the other side?" Karl asks from the rock I should be standing on. My knees sway in the moving water; the creek nudges my waist. I paw at the air with my free hand, trying to keep my balance, and nearly topple over. This stupid backpack!

Karl's grip tightens. Like I'm a toddler who can't be left alone in a swimming pool without his plastic floaties.

With his other hand, Karl loops the gun strap over his head, making the strap fit diagonally across his chest with his gun across his back.

"Walk across!" Dad shouts from the shore.

The muscles in my legs quiver as I attempt to fight the moving water. I finally manage to move my leg and wedge my shoe against something hard on the creek bed, forcing my balance. I wrench from Karl's grip.

"Slow and steady," he instructs.

I carefully shift my weight and plant my other foot between a pair of rocks. And then I do it again. Karl remains on the rock as I slog through the water—my thighs burn with each slow stride—until I finally slosh onto the bank.

On this side of the creek, the trees have been cleared. I shiver from the sudden breeze. The moon gives off just enough light where I can see the concern lining Dad's face. He probably thinks bringing me here was a mistake. I know that's what *I'm* thinking.

I can't believe I thought I could actually help him, or that I could actually make him *like* me. I can't even cross a stupid creek without screwing it up. My bottom lip trembles.

All of a sudden, Dad's hand lands on my shoulder. The unexpected weight surprises and steadies me.

"I'm sorry," I whisper.

Karl clears his throat as he lands behind me. "We're in the home stretch," he says before moving uphill.

Great, more climbing.

Without warning, Dad removes the bag; my shoulders automatically rise. "Can you make it a little longer?" he asks, holding my wet backpack.

I nod, because it's easier than crying.

Dad follows Karl, carrying both bug-out bags with ease.

My dripping clothes hang from my body, and I'm pretty sure I smell like dead fish. But I keep climbing, determined not to disappoint Dad again.

My socks squish with each step until we finally reach a level area where there's a two-story plywood cabin.

Tree branches wrap around the structure, almost like a web of arms supporting it. It looks like nobody's been here in a long, long time. A soft mechanical hum charges the air.

Light filters through the black curtains on the cabin windows. I breathe. There's electricity. But how?

The hum seems to grow louder. "Generator?" I ask, swiping the wet hair from my face. Yep, I definitely smell like dead fish.

Karl nods. "In the shed," he says, pointing. "Back there."

I can barely see the outline of a smaller plywood structure tucked behind the cabin.

I wring the water from the bottom of my T-shirt. "Gas or propane?"

Karl's questioning gaze shifts to Dad.

Dad shakes his head. "Kid's into mechanical stuff," he says, stomping up the steps to an uneven wraparound porch.

Karl crosses his arms over his chest. "Solar with a propane backup."

"Nice," I say, rubbing my hands together, trying to keep my fingers warm. "Where are the panels?"

"Can we go inside?" Dad asks, interrupting.

Karl nears the door. "Of course."

The creek is quieter from up here, lulling and soothing. Damp exhaustion suddenly hits, making me yawn.

"You need to change clothes before you catch cold," Dad says, sounding a little like Mom used to.

I nod.

"Everything should be in order," Karl says as he leads him inside.

My gaze moves up, up, up for a second, up through the black network of branches overhead until I spot the stars winking down at me. Maybe things will be okay after all.

The boards on the porch creak beneath my wet shoes. Inside, there's a set of stairs to my immediate right, leading to an open loft with a simple railing. The first floor is about the size of our den in Amarillo, but with a tiny kitchen, a table and chairs, and a futon shoved at the rear of the cabin. Above the futon is a sign with a red circle around the words: NEW WORLD ORDER. A diagonal line cuts through the middle of the circle.

There it is again. "What's the New World Order?" I ask.

Dad shakes his head. "I'm sorry," he says to Karl before facing me. "I've told you: It's the group that's trying to impose a global government. And once it does, the New World Order plans to turn the world's population into its slaves."

I think I would've remembered if he'd told me something like that. I eye him, suspicious, expecting him to say, "Just kidding." He doesn't.

"And the federal government is in on it." Dad turns to Karl. "Right?"

Karl gives a stiff nod.

Apparently, they actually believe this stuff.

Dad points to a blue-and-white-checkered cloth strung across a sagging rope along the rear wall. "What's behind the curtain?"

"Bathroom," Karl says.

"Water safe to drink?"

Karl turns the tap in the kitchen. Clear water streams from the faucet. "Ought to be. It's spring-fed."

A smile tugs at the corner of Dad's mouth. Sudden warmth—the good kind—settles inside my chest. It's been a long time since I've seen him smile like that.

"A little better than what you had over there, huh?" Karl asks, shutting off the tap.

No, don't ruin this. Don't remind him of his tours of duty.

Dad nods. "A little."

"You'll probably be more comfortable upstairs, then," Karl notes, pointing to the loft. "There's a full-sized mattress."

"You serious?" Dad says, his smile widening as if Karl told him he'd won a lifetime subscription to *Field & Stream* magazine. Dad grabs his gun cases and the bug-out bags, taking the stairs two at a time with his arms full.

Our boxes line the kitchen countertop and table.

Karl inches toward the front door. "Need anything else?"

I spot my comics and then my crate with QUEN-10. Suddenly, I think of the competition. And my message across the lockers. The look on Ajeet's face.

Only a little bit of red paint remains crusted along the edges of my fingernails. My insides twist. I take off my soggy hoodie and toss it into the stainless sink with a *splat*.

"Still cold?" Karl asks.

"Nope," I say, leaving puddles behind me as I walk across the raw wooden floor. If Aunt Birdie were here, she'd yell at me to clean up my mess. I'd roll my eyes as she made me clean up after myself, telling me I missed a spot. But there's no one here to fuss over my messes now.

I lift QUEN-10 from the crate, wishing I could turn back time. I push the power button. The battery is still dead.

"Everything alright?" Karl asks, his voice a little softer.

Dad stomps around upstairs. Probably finding the perfect hiding spot for his guns.

"Needs a charge," I say, pointing to my robot.

Karl looks at me, like he's expecting me to say something more—like he wants to know my secrets—but I press my lips together. That's all you're going to get from me.

"Very well," Karl says as he opens the door; the wind moves through the trees.

I rifle through the crate until I find a cable and then an outlet behind the table. I crouch and plug my robot into the wall. The light flashes red—the battery is charging.

"Good night, then," Karl says, his loud voice filling the cabin.

Dad grunts a response from upstairs.

"See you in the morning," Karl adds.

I search another crate, checking to see if Dad packed my spare battery. As I'm wading through the wires and parts, my brain suddenly alerts that I didn't hear the door shut.

Karl is standing in the doorway, still staring at me like he's assessing something. Or someone.

QUEN-10 slips from my hand, and I nearly drop him. "Is there something else?" I ask. I glance toward the loft but don't see Dad.

"I was waiting for your response," Karl answers.

I shift, uneasy. "To what?"

"See you in the morning."

"Me?" My voice shakes a little. Real smooth.

"You are an excellent marksman, right?"

QUEN-10 rattles in my hands.

He gives me a half-hearted salute. "See you at weapons training."

Before I can react, my robot hits the floor, shattering into pieces.

NINE

The next morning, my fingers brush across the broken pieces of QUEN-10 on the table. I lift my phone from the charger and groan. No service. No Wi-Fi. Aunt Birdie is going to be so worried. Frustrated, I toss my phone onto the table.

My stomach growls as I huff into the kitchen and, one by one, open the kitchen cabinets and refrigerator looking for something to eat, only to slam them all shut. Nothing but a box of Dad's protein bars. I snatch one from the box on the countertop and move outside onto the wraparound porch, gobbling the cardboard-tasting bar in three bites.

The early-morning light has turned the leaves bright green; they tremble in the breeze. I rub my aching knee, careful to avoid the sticky gash where it struck the rock last night. I breathe in the smell of dirt and wood. It's so peaceful here.

Dad stomps from the cabin onto the porch, startling me. He's wearing camo fatigues, his face tight as he covers his eyes with reflective shades. There's a black assault rifle slung across his chest. He clomps down the stairs, checking the magazine on his handgun for bullets before shoving the gun into a holster on his hip.

So much for peaceful.

"When can we go fishing?" I ask, pointing over the edge of the slope to the creek bubbling softly below. I know they're in there because I still smell like fish after falling into the water last night.

"Later," Dad says, adjusting the knife inside his boot. "Let's go." Dad walks around the side of the cabin and out of view.

"Dad," I call as I follow him, slip-sliding down the hill.

He stalls, waiting for me by the edge of the creek.

I can't really see his eyes behind the shades, which actually helps me ask the question I've been meaning to ask: "You didn't really tell them I'm an excellent marksman, did you?"

Dad turns his head and chews his bottom lip. The only sound is the flowing water. Bad sign.

"You didn't," I whisper.

He rubs the brown stubble along the sides of his face. "Look. I didn't have any choice, okay?" He shifts the rifle on his chest. "The point is I wanted you with me. That should count for something, right?"

"So you told them I knew how to shoot?" I don't know why I'm so surprised. Of course he told them what he wanted me to be. Not what I really am.

He clears his throat and looks away again. "I didn't think they'd let me bring you if I didn't tell them something."

And I guess the truth wasn't good enough. "You know I don't know how." It's all I can do to keep from hurling at the thought. "I haven't touched a gun since—" I stop myself from going there. I can't.

"Maybe it's time you get over that."

Seriously? *That's* the best he can do?

He lets out a hard sigh. "Most boys would love the chance to shoot with their dads."

I want to say: *In case you haven't noticed, I'm not "most boys." I don't like football. I don't like guns. Why can't you see that's not me?* But I don't say those things. I can't.

His gaze wanders to the other side of the creek. "Part of the idea in coming here was to try new things."

"I know," I say, followed by a sigh. But I thought *new things* meant not showering for days without having to listen to Aunt Birdie complain about the stink. Maybe even riding four-wheelers or roasting marshmallows over a campfire like

Mom and I used to do. I didn't think it meant me having to shoot a gun.

"I'll teach you," he says. "And if you don't like it, you can quit."

"Promise?" I ask quickly. I guess too quickly.

His face falls. "We're late." Dad turns and leaps across the water, landing on the exposed rock in the center of the creek and then on the other side. He pauses there, impatiently gripping the rifle against his chest.

I carefully hop to the dry rock in the center before meeting him on the bank.

"That wasn't so bad, was it?" Dad asks, talking to me like I'm four years old.

I swallow hard. This is why I don't try to talk to him.

Of course it wasn't so bad. *Today.* In the daylight when I can actually see where I'm going and when there's not some Nazi-looking dude, threatening me with a gun.

But I know better than to say anything: Dad doesn't care about those kinds of details.

The distant pop of gunfire makes us both jump.

Dad curses and grasps his rifle like a madman in one of those war movies. He rushes downhill. Toward the sound. Why is he moving *toward* the gunfire?

Every instinct in my body tells me to turn and run. Dad

comes to a sudden stop and glances over his shoulder, gesturing for me to follow. If I run the opposite direction, he'll be so mad. "Come on," he urges.

He asked me to come; I'm here. If we're not ever together, how can I help him?

I shove my fists into the pockets of my hoodie and follow. We slip-slide downhill through the thick trees, the echoes of gunfire growing louder. Dad stops several feet short of the clearing. Men shout commands. It smells like gunpowder and ammonia.

"Here," Dad says, handing me a pair of fluorescent-orange earplugs. He taps the blue ones in his ears. "You'll still be able to hear, but they'll help protect your eardrums."

I follow his lead, squeezing the plugs inside my ears. They rapidly expand, muffling the booming echo of gunshots.

"Ready?" he asks.

No, I think. "Yes."

Together, we exit the cover of trees and move into the wide clearing. Men in fatigues run though an obstacle course. Inside the maze, Wade drops behind a stack of tires, taking cover. His shiny scar stretches along his neck as he peeks over the wall of tires and, one by one, blows the heads off a straw family. *Boom, boom, boom, BOOM!*

I startle with each shot.

On the other side of the clearing, there's a line of kids in camo—boys and girls, ranging anywhere from seven to seventeen-years-old. Karl, the creepy, Nazi-looking guy, supervises them as they shoot flat, human-shaped paper targets.

"There are kids here?" I say, surprised.

Dad nods. "Wade says, with it being almost summertime, you'll see them here more over the next few weeks."

I shift uncomfortably. There's so many of them already. It looks like these guys are training an army.

In the very center of the group of kids, a girl with a pair of blond braids turns and stares at us. About my age, she's wearing large, headphone-style ear protection and a tan, military-style vest. For some reason, I decide to copy Connor Green's cool, one-finger wave hello.

The girl smirks and pulls a gun from her vest. My heart leaps to my throat as she spins toward the target and fires, hitting the center of its forehead, then its nose, and finally its heart. I wipe my hands on my jeans.

"You're late, soldier!" Wade yells over the noise. His pink, puckered scar glistens in the sunlight.

"I'm sorry, sir," Dad says. "Won't happen again."

"My fault. I overslept," I say, trying to take the heat off Dad.

"We both did." He slaps my shoulder. "It was a long trip."

I nod. Yes, we're on the same team.

"Well then, I guess you're next," Wade says.

"Next?" I ask as Dad gives a stiff nod.

Wade's dark eyes narrow. "Cease fire!" he yells, his voice reverberating through the woods. Within a few seconds, the gunfire stops. The world goes quiet.

The dry leaves crackle beneath Wade's boots as he nears. With him this close, I can see the white lines running through the pinkish scar along his face and throat. It continues beneath his shirt and spreads out from under his sleeve onto his right hand. My stomach turns as he leans over me. "Where's your weapon, son?"

My mouth goes dry. "Uh." The wind picks up; the trees creak around us.

Dwight, the Chewbacca look-alike, approaches. "Your son didn't bring a gun?"

My eyes fall to my running shoes. "I forgot," I lie.

"Doesn't he know it's disrespectful to look away from a senior commander?" Wade asks.

I bite my lip. I'm embarrassing Dad already when I promised myself I wouldn't. I look at Wade, straight into his sharp eyes. Sweat beads on my forehead.

He's gripping the tan gun strapped across his chest and

spits into the dirt, like he knows how dry my mouth is. "I hope you realize how lucky you are to be here."

I bite my tongue, hoping to force it to make spit.

Wade gestures at the line of kids. "These are the next generation of Flag Bearers. They come here to learn from the best."

By "the best," I'm assuming he means Karl, who was supervising them seconds before and is glaring at me now.

Wade paces. "We come to learn how to fight and defeat the New World Order." Leaves crunch beneath his boots as he yells, "The white race is under attack! We are here to end the assault on our culture by these animals the government's now calling *immigrants*."

I cringe. Aren't most Americans immigrants or at least the descendants of immigrants?

Wade stops in place, hovering over me. His breath smells like garlic and something sour. "We're here to prepare for the revolution," he says before shouting, "Who watches the watchmen?"

The entire camp responds, "WE DO!"

"*Who?*"

"WE DO!"

I'm hoping Dad can see how crazy this guy is, but he's nodding along.

"Morgan," Wade calls.

All of a sudden, the scary girl with the braids hurries to his side. "Yes, Daddy."

My hands clench. Figures this one is his daughter.

"Boy needs to borrow a gun," Wade says, his voice oily. "Seems to have forgotten his own."

Morgan stares at me for a second, like she's sizing me up. Her eyes are blue as the sky. They're kind of pretty and frightening all at the same time.

I try Connor's wave again. "I'm Rebel," I say, my voice squeaking on the last syllable.

She sneers, making me feel like the total idiot I am. "Come on," she says, sounding annoyed as she turns her back on me and nears the line of targets.

Dad gestures for me to follow her. But I thought *he* was going to be the one to teach me. *Go,* he mouths.

Somehow, I manage to move my feet. Maybe Dad gave me a little push. I wipe my fingers against my hoodie.

Kids part as I near the platform. It's about chest-high with a rifle that looks like Dad's AR-15 propped on the flat surface. My heart thrums.

A human-shaped target with red lines and circles stands about the length of five robotics tables from the platform.

Morgan is to my right. Karl to my left. The woods rustle behind me; everyone else presses in on me.

My knee bangs the metal stool in front of the platform. Pain shoots down my leg as the scab rips open. I bite my lip to keep from crying out.

"Shot one of these before?" Karl asks.

I quickly shake my head.

"It's been a while," Dad corrects.

But he's wrong. It wasn't like this one. It was a bolt-action rifle, bigger than this. And I was hoping I'd never have to think about it ever again.

"Center up," Dad instructs.

For the millionth time, I wish he'd be happy with me being me. Instead, he's hovering behind my right shoulder, nodding with suffocating encouragement.

Karl taps the top of the gun. "You can keep it on the table or carry it, whichever you prefer."

I eye the big black killing machine I'm supposed to touch now. There's no way I'm picking this thing up. My hands are already shaking. I weakly slide onto the stool. But that doesn't keep the rest of me from trembling. I clench and unclench my hands. It's hard to breathe. There are too many people. Too many guns.

"Whenever you're ready," Karl prompts.

"Shoot the damn gun already," Wade says.

Morgan snorts a giggle, reminding me of Ajeet.

Chill bumps race along my sweaty arms. I close my eyes and hastily pull the trigger. Nothing. I pull again. Nothing.

"Might help if you flip the safety," Wade says from over my left shoulder. Everyone laughs; I can sense Dad shrinking behind me.

"Come on, Rebel," he barks. "Quit joking around."

I stiffen and what I really want to do is spin around and tell him: *So I'm a joke now, too? Because I'd rather go fishing than fire one of these things again? I know what a gun can do!*

"Safety's there," a tall, skinny boy with acne and a huge overbite says as he reaches around Karl and points to the left side of the gun.

"He knows where it is," Dad insists.

But I don't. Or, at least, I didn't. "Thanks," I whisper to the boy.

"Don't mention it. Name's Justin by the way." He gives me a goofy grin. Like we're meeting at GameStop and not in the middle of a band of armed racists. "You play *Minecraft*?" he asks, pointing at the pixelated Creepers on my T-shirt.

I nod, my hands slipping from the gun.

"What console do you have?"

"Xbox."

"Cool," he says. "I play on a Wii U."

Yikes. Not one of Nintendo's finer moments.

"Enough!" Wade barks.

Justin drops his head like a scolded puppy; he suddenly won't look at me. "Flip it when you're ready," he adds, pointing blindly to the safety.

The tremors in my hands return as my fingers move from the table to the weapon. I carefully flip the black switch and hold my breath, forcing myself still.

Karl touches my shoulder. My breath escapes my chest as he pushes me toward the gun. "I think you need to wrap around it a little more this time," he says.

The gun presses into my shoulder. Blood beats inside my ears. My finger slowly slips in next to the trigger.

"Left hand down a little," Karl instructs. "Eyes open."

I'm light-headed.

"Look through the ACOG for your target."

I don't know what that means. Every nerve in my body is on alert.

I hold my breath and *bang!* There's a loud echo, pulsing through the woods. Pulsing through me. My ears ring. Tears sting the backs of my eyes. My whole body's shaking. I can't even force myself still. I stand, wanting to get away from it.

My earplugs muffle people's screams.

Fear seizes Morgan's eyes. I'm practically convulsing.

"What the hell are you doing?" Wade asks and snatches the gun from my hands.

I didn't realize I'd pulled it off the platform.

"You never point a gun at somebody you don't intend to shoot!" He switches the safety and slams the gun onto the table. I flinch as he turns to Dad. "I thought you said this boy knew about guns."

My pulse races; Dad won't look at me.

"Boy's a disgrace," Wade adds. "Look at him."

Dad follows orders. He looks, and I can see the shame in his eyes.

Morgan jabs her finger into my chest, forcing me to stumble. Her face is tight with fury. "You could've killed me, jerk!"

I grit my teeth, forcing back tears. She's right. And that's exactly the problem.

Before anyone can stop me, I spin toward the trees and run.

TEN

I dash between the tree trunks, yanking the earplugs from my ears and letting them drop to the ground. My breath comes in short gasps. Narrow branches crisscross before me, but I keep pushing forward. Green leaves reach from the twigs, brushing and tickling the skin on my face and arms, taunting me.

The creek rages in front of me. The sun glares from between the trees. I stop before I cross, daring to look. But no one's there. No one's chasing me. Especially not Dad.

Why can't I have a *normal* relationship with him? Most dads I know shoot hoops, not guns. They watch football or play video games with their sons.

My fingers curl inside my hoodie; I dry my eyes on my sleeve. What now?

My body's trembling. Too many nerves. Too many words pinned inside my brain. Too many memories.

I shake my head. I don't want to think about any of that now.

Gunfire begins to pop again in the clearing. I have to keep moving.

After crossing the creek, I follow the curve and bend of the water, away from our cabin on the hill. Boulders jut from the ground between dried leaves. Clover-shaped lichen swallows the rocks and crawls around the tree trunks. Branches lay scattered and broken at my feet.

Sweat beads along my forehead and trickles down my back the longer I walk until I finally take off my hoodie and tie the arms around my waist. But I don't stop.

Touching the damp and spongy lichen, I climb over the waist-high boulders until, eventually, the trees thin around another bend in the creek and the water flows down a small waterfall.

From the top, I peek over the edge. There's a wall of rocks next to the waterfall, leading to a smaller stream.

I slowly and carefully descend the rocks. Mist from the waterfall dampens my face as I use each rock like a stairstep until landing at the base.

The creek is calmer down here. Clearer. Fish swim along

the center of the stream in groups. Their iridescent fins glow as they catch the glittering sunlight through the branches on the overhanging trees.

I follow the fish a few feet downstream, twigs snapping beneath my feet. The breeze sighs through the leaves. There's the smell of something sweet.

"You look lost," a girl's voice says, stopping me in my tracks.

I immediately duck behind the nearest tree trunk, scanning the woods behind me.

Light laughter echoes along the creek. "Do you think I can't see you now?"

My fingernails dig into the peeling bark as my gaze slips around the narrow trunk until I find her: a girl, fishing on the other side of the creek. She smiles and waves.

I stiffen, because her skin is black. Doesn't she know about the Flag Bearers? What would they do if they found her? What would they do to me? I scoot from my hiding place and immediately tumble over a fallen branch, smacking my messed-up knee against sharp wood.

Heat spreads throughout my body. My fingers dig into the ground, crunching handfuls of leaves before I angrily toss them in the air. Why are there so many stupid things to trip on?

"So, are you?" She casts the red bobber on the end of her fishing line into the creek with a *plunk*.

In spite of the pain, I rise, brushing off my jeans. "Am I what?" I grunt.

"Lost."

I shake my head and limp toward the wall of rocks, ready to climb them and disappear.

"You don't have to go, you know. What's your name?"

Out of habit, I answer.

She eyes my *Minecraft* T-shirt and laughs a little, making me instantly regret answering.

"How old are you, *Rebel*?" she asks, pronouncing my name like she's making fun.

"Thirteen," I say, defensively folding my arms over the Creepers on my chest. "How old are you?"

"Thirteen and a half." She raises her chin like she's one-upped me.

I scoff. We stopped counting half years when we were in kindergarten. "And your name?"

She props the end of the fishing pole against the hip of her jeans; the line swishes to the right. "Calliope."

I snort. "And you think *my* name is bad."

Her nose wrinkles, and I almost regret insulting her, because it's actually a nice name. But then she jams her fishing pole into the mud alongside the bank, leaving the bobber floating on the water's surface.

With both hands, Calliope tugs on the hem of her shirt and starts downstream. I assume she's walking away so I don't see her cry, but then I realize she's nearing a fallen log that bridges the water between us.

What's she doing?

She steps onto the log.

Oh, no.

Within seconds, her red sneakers are scooting sideways across the fallen tree and moving toward my side of the creek.

Oh, God. She can't come over.

I glance uphill, toward the Flag Bearers. "I take it back," I say, nearing the waterfall. "Your name's awesome." I try to get a foothold on the damp rock and slip. This didn't seem so steep before. My hands are too sweaty to get a good grip. I try again and actually find my footing, climbing a bit before slipping again. I really should've gone to that wall-climbing place when Ajeet asked.

"At least I'm named after the goddess of epic poetry," she says.

I check over my shoulder. She's now on my side of the bank, nearing with her hands on her hips, the way Aunt Birdie sometimes does.

I manage to scale a few more rocks.

"For your information, Calliope was one of the nine muses in Greek mythology." She stops beneath me at the base of the rock staircase, glaring at me. Her hair is an angry spray of curls around her face. "Who are you supposed to be named after?"

I stop climbing for a second. I'd never really thought about it before.

"Because you sure don't look like a *rebel* to me, especially in that shirt." She lets out a dry laugh. "I mean, no offense, but what thirteen-year-old still wears a *Minecraft* T-shirt?"

My face goes hot. "My mom gave it to me." It was way too big for me then, and now it barely fits.

Calliope grins, her teeth white like a toothpaste commercial. She's making fun of me.

I face the rocks and run my tongue across my gritty teeth.

"Did you know the Navajo attribute powers to their names?" she says, completely random. "Like a name may be considered so precious it's only used during ceremonies."

What's she talking about?

"So, a conversation may go something like, 'Father, ask daughter for bread.'"

"That's nice," I say, my breath huffing as I resume climbing.

"Can you imagine how confusing that could get?" She snaps her fingers. "Oh, and traditionally Hawaiian families believed an ancestral god would deliver a name to an unborn child's family through visions or dreams."

"Uh-huh," I mutter. Who *is* this girl?

"Names are pretty important," she says as I finally reach the top of the waterfall.

My chest heaves, short of breath. "Yeah—well, I don't know what my name means—so . . ." I scowl down at her for ruining my perfectly good walk. For making fun of the shirt my mom gave me. For hating my name, which was actually one of the few things I halfway liked about myself.

She looks up at me without flinching. My face heats. She wouldn't be so confident if she saw Wade and all his armed Flag Bearers.

I clench my fists, barking, "Don't follow me if you know what's good for you." My voice cracks on the last word. Of course it does.

She scoffs.

My neck prickles. I can't even make a threat without screwing it up.

I march the opposite direction.

"Where are you going?" Calliope calls from the base of the waterfall.

My feet keep moving, but this time I'm careful, watching for downed branches. I glance over my shoulder every few seconds, expecting her to pop over the edge of the rocks. But there's nothing but an army of trees. I huff, convincing myself the threat worked. That's right: Don't follow me.

I continue along the creek when my stomach growls, nagging me. I really should've thought this through before I left. I'm not a hunter, *obviously*. And it's not like I've ever foraged for berries. I haven't seen any berries and, even if I did, I wouldn't know if they were poisonous. The only other option is tree bark, but that's a hard pass. I can only imagine the splinters on the way out.

I sigh, knowing I have to go back to the cabin.

About a half hour later, I'm slip-sliding up the gentle slope to reach it. The porch steps creak beneath my feet and, with a breath, I open the door.

"Dad," I call.

Nothing but the gentle hum of the generator.

The cabin smells musty, unlived in. I open and close the cabinets again, but they're still empty. I snatch another protein bar from the box, gobbling the tasteless, glue-like glob. After a few gulps of water from the sink faucet, I'm still hungry and dreaming of real food.

Think, think. I spot my phone charging on the table, and wonder if there's pizza delivery out here. With sudden, desperate thoughts of doughy crust, tangy sauce, and melty cheese, I grab my phone. My mouth waters as the screen brightens, but there's still no service. No Wi-Fi. Nothing.

Heat surges through me. I pound the table with my fist; QUEN-10's parts bounce and scatter.

There has to be food around here someplace.

I throw my useless phone against the table, shattering the screen. *Holy!* I have to get out of here. I storm outside and slam the cabin door shut.

The sun tilts in the sky; it's probably after noon. My stomach grumbles, mocking me again.

"Fine!" I yell to the woods. "Fine!" I yell even louder, scratching my throat. "I'll go look for him. Is that what you want?"

The only answer I get is the whine of mosquitos swarming the porch. I swat the air and move from the cloud of bugs before managing a breath. And then two breaths.

"Fine," I say to myself and move downhill and across the river, trudging through the thick trees.

I'm soon at the clearing again, where I almost shot Morgan. I swallow the lump in my throat.

The sound of gunfire is gone. The smell of gunpowder and ammonia, gone. Birds call to one another from the branches, one high-pitched and sharp, another like a low thrum.

Where is everybody? Then, I remember the watchtower. My gaze darts to the wooden structure overhead. Empty.

"Hello?" I say.

No answer.

Slowly, I leave the cover of trees and move past the obstacle course, the straw men's heads scattered on the ground. I slip past the shooting range, the paper bodies shredded by kids' bullets.

As I creep toward the FLAG BEARERS WHITES ONLY sign on the side of the gray building, I hear a man's voice coming from inside. I edge around the long side of the structure to the end, where the gravelly voice grows louder: "We're heading into a revolution. It's time to stand up like men and slaughter our enemy."

It sounds like Wade.

"We need to take our country back from those soulless coloreds and reclaim our way of life that's under attack."

I think of how I hurt Ajeet and cringe. He wasn't soulless.

"It's time to destroy those who would sully our bloodlines and the so-called government that supports them."

I wonder if Dad's in there, listening. I scoot around the corner of the building and duck next to a pair of screened-in doors.

"Death to the New World Order!"

Men shout and holler their approval.

"Hear anything good?" a voice whispers.

I look up; my heart drums when I see his rigid face.

ELEVEN

"Karl," I choke, looking up at the head of security.

He clutches the gun slung across his broad chest. "And here I thought you had enough sense to get out of here."

I gulp. "I came back," I say, stupidly stating the obvious.

"Ah, there you are," Dwight says as he rounds the building. "All clear on that side." He stops short when he spots me and then grins his Chewbacca grin at Karl. "You were right."

"About what?" I ask, looking between them. The back of my head slowly slides up the side of the building until I'm standing, but still several inches shorter than both of them.

Karl's expression tightens. "That you'd come crawling back."

Dwight runs a hand under his baseball cap. His shaggy hair sticks out over his ears. "What should we do with him?"

"What do you think?" Karl snaps. "Take him to Wade."

"I'm good," I say, my voice weak, but they're already nudging me toward the door.

Through the screen, I can see Wade standing in the center of a circle of about twelve seated men. The room is dark, except for the beam of light surrounding Wade. "We must draw our enemies into the sea. We are the last of the patriots! We must—"

The door creaks as I'm shoved inside. Wade stops ranting when he notices us in the doorway.

Dad rises from one of the chairs in the circle. "Rebel?" It's hard to tell in the dim light, but I think he looks relieved to see me.

I manage a breath. "Hi."

"So," Wade says. "The coward returns."

I flinch.

Some of the men chuckle, while high-pitched snickers come from the far side of the room. I squint, spotting the kids from earlier. They're seated beyond the circle of men.

Wade gestures for me to come into the circle. "You're just in time to witness your father take the oath."

The oath?

My legs wobble as Dwight and Karl guide me to the edge of the circle of chairs.

Dad straightens to attention.

"Your father is quite the marksman," Wade says over his men. "He made a kill with a single shot on every target. Five times in a row."

I suppose that should make me proud, but my stomach tightens instead.

Dad stands expressionless.

Wade lifts a thin eyebrow, the one on the scarred side of his face. "Bring the boy inside the circle."

I shake my head, trying to dig the soles of my shoes into the concrete.

"Don't resist," Karl whispers. "You'll be safer if you do as he says."

Safer? I shake my head again, but it's no use. With Karl behind me, I'm walking whether I want to or not.

"Children," Wade announces. "Apparently this boy needs some encouragement. Won't you join him in the patriot's circle?"

Chairs scoot against the floor, and the children, led by Morgan, are funneling between men into the center.

"Go," Karl says under his breath, nudging me.

I glance at his gun and move, wedging between two men in order to reach the center of the circle. Small hands pull me by my arms through the group until I'm standing in front of Dad.

He stares at some fixed point behind me.

There's a reassuring pat on my shoulder. I glance over, and it's Justin, smiling at me.

"This!" Wade shouts, pointing to the center of the circle. "Is the future of the Aryan race!"

"Here, here!" most of the men chant.

Wade walks the full circle between the men and us. "Nathan Mercer."

"Yes, sir," Dad answers, short and loud, like he's answering a true commanding officer.

Wade stops when he reaches us. "Are you ready to take the oath of the Flag Bearers?"

"Yes, sir," Dad says without hesitation.

I swallow hard.

"Then repeat after me," Wade instructs. "I make this covenant in my own blood."

Dad parrots the words, almost like he's in a trance.

This isn't happening. I thought the point of us coming here was for him to get better. For us to get better.

"I will honor this brotherhood," Dad repeats. "And enter into a full state of war against the government of the United States and all those who support it."

My knees buckle; I stumble into Justin.

"Watch it," he whispers.

Dad continues, "I promise to fight for a pure, white nation, as our founding fathers intended."

No, this is wrong. These people are wrong. "Dad," I say under my breath, trying to get him to snap out of it. Even if it means getting Angry Dad, I'd rather have that than this.

But he keeps going: "I promise not to lay down my weapons until we prevail."

My gaze darts across the white faces of the kids and men in the room. I should say something, but I can't. Most of the men are grasping their guns. Blood beats inside my ears.

"I solemnly swear to live and die for the Flag Bearers."

Die?

"So help me God."

Wade salutes my dad. "Welcome aboard, soldier."

"Thank you, sir." Dad returns the salute and shakes Wade's scarred hand.

When he releases my dad, Wade calls his men to attention. All of them jump from their chairs, guns at their sides, standing perfectly still.

The kids around me smile and nod with pride. My stomach curdles.

I shouldn't be here. This is *wrong*. We shouldn't be here.

"Who watches the watchmen?" Wade barks.

"WE DO!"

Wade grins at his small army. "Then let the battle begin."

***

I can't stop thinking about the oath. He'd fight against our government; he'd fight for an all-white nation. How could Dad make those promises?

It's late in the afternoon, and we're driving the switchbacks down the mountain. Normally, I'd be happy inside Dad's truck, heading toward the real world in order to finally get some real food. But I'm surrounded by militiamen. Dwight sits next to me in the back seat; Wade sits in the front with Dad driving.

Wade insisted on all of us going to the convenience store to get food for our cabin. I don't know why. It's like he refuses to leave Dad and me alone.

My stomach growls. Wade drums his fingers on the door as our truck sways side to side. "Did you pack the bandannas?" he asks.

Dad's shoulders stiffen as he reaches the base of the mountain and pulls onto the main highway.

"Yep," Dwight answers through a wad of tobacco. His hairy body is hunched over as he tinkers with a disassembled AR-15 on his lap. He struggles with one of the parts.

The rest of the parts lay on a towel between us. I scoot as far away from him as I can, my left leg pressed against the door, while he jams a large, key-shaped piece in and out of another section of the gun. "Dangit!" he says, bumping his head against the ceiling of the truck. "I can't get the stupid charging assembly in the upper."

Wade glances over the front seat, showing the clear profile of his face without the scar. "What's your problem?"

Dwight pulls a white Styrofoam cup from his door and spits, adding to the brown sludge at the bottom. My stomach turns as he wipes his bottom lip with his hand. "I cleaned my gun, and now I can't get it back together."

Wade faces forward. "Moron." He and Dad laugh.

"Here," Dwight says, holding the parts over the seat in front of him. "You think it's so easy? You try it."

"Rebel, why don't you take a look?" Dad says, glancing at me in the rearview mirror.

Me? But I don't want to touch another gun. I can't.

Wade scoffs, like he doesn't believe I can do it.

I scan the parts; my breath goes shallow as I remember the feel of the rifle against my cheek. The loud *bang*. The blood.

"Rebel!" Dad barks, yanking me out of the past. His gaze switches from the road to the rearview mirror a few times.

"Y-yes, sir," I answer, forcing my hands to stop shaking.

Dwight scoots the tobacco to the other side of his mouth with his tongue and hands over the black parts he was calling "upper" and the large, key-shaped part he was calling the "charging assembly."

I take a breath and examine the charging assembly for a second, telling myself it's only engineering. Like robotics. Just another problem that needs to be solved.

Then I close one eye, peeking down the hole of the upper, searching for the space where the tooth of the key should fit. I think I've spotted it and slide the key inside the hole and push toward the top, feeling the tooth click into the notch. I nod, satisfied. Okay, this isn't so bad. It's almost like building with oversized Legos.

"How'd you do that?" Dwight asks, spitting in his cup.

I smile without answering and glance at the remaining parts spread between us on the seat. I grab the rounded one and hold it out to him. "What's this one called?" I ask, the part cold between my fingers.

"Bolt carrier assembly. How'd you know that's next?"

Because this is like building with Legos, finding the parts that click. I shrug. "I like putting stuff together." I slide the bolt carrier assembly inside the chamber where I'd inserted the key.

"This kid's a natural," Dwight says.

Dad nods. "Told you."

My chest swells a little.

I can feel Wade watching as I grab the lower part with the trigger and align the pins of the newly assembled upper with the lower before finally latching them together with a *click, click.* "Done," I say, handing it to Dwight.

"Not bad," Wade says.

Dwight puts a hand on the seat in front of him. "Maybe we should put the kid on the assembly line."

In the rearview mirror, I spot Dad smiling at me.

I breathe. I actually did something right for a change.

Dwight digs the brass bullets from the seat pocket in front of him. I shift in my seat, pointing to the newly assembled gun. "Why do you carry a gun everywhere?"

Dad's shoulders retighten. Wade glares at me. So much for doing something right.

"Because it's my right to carry it," Dwight says, returning the bullets to the seat pocket as he faces me. "And the New World Order is trying to take it away."

"Damn straight," Dad says with a nod.

Dwight spits the tobacco wad into his cup—the lump of brown bobs and floats in its juices—before he returns the cup to the door. He pulls a dollar bill from his wallet. "Look at this," he says, pushing it toward me.

I take the warm, wrinkled dollar bill in my hand, faceup. George Washington looks at me like he has a secret.

"Flip it over," Dwight instructs.

I flip it over in my hand, scanning for a clue. A pyramid. IN GOD WE TRUST. An eagle. I shrug. "So?"

"See the eye over the pyramid?"

I spot the glowing eye in the triangle above the pyramid and nod.

"That's a sign."

I smirk. "What do you mean?"

"America has been taken over by secret forces. They've taken control of the Federal Reserve."

I snort an awkward laugh and immediately cover my mouth.

"You wait." Dwight snatches the dollar bill from me and stuffs it inside his wallet. "You won't be laughing when they come after you." He switches his gun to the other hand, looking like he wants to shoot me.

I'm just happy he's forgotten the bullets are still inside the seat pocket.

"Here we are," Wade says.

Dwight stops glaring at me as Dad turns into the parking lot and pulls up to a plain brown brick building with the peeling red-and-white sign: DAIRY MART & GAS.

We hop from the truck. "I'll keep watch," Dwight grunts, unrolling his window.

All of a sudden, I notice how dirty Dad's truck is. The license plates and doors are covered with mud. Strange. Dad usually keeps his truck so clean you can eat off the hood. I'm almost positive it didn't get this dirty on the drive up and down the mountain. "We could get a car wash while we're here," I offer.

Dad looks at Wade and then opens the convenience store door; a bell rings. "Maybe," Dad says as I start to feel the air-conditioning. It smells like popcorn and fried burritos. My stomach gurgles with hunger.

Out of nowhere, there's a loud, high-pitched whistle. Dad jumps before tensing. We both turn toward the sound.

Next to the nearest gas pump, a man in a black T-shirt and camo pants pulls his index fingers from his lips. He's wearing the same clothes the Flag Bearers wear at camp, but he doesn't look familiar.

Wade gives us a nod. "Y'all go on in. I'll be right back."

Dad shuts the glass door but doesn't move, his hand squeezing the handle tight. He's sweating a little as he spies on Wade, who's approaching the guy at the gas pumps.

"You okay?" I ask.

Dad clears his throat. "Let's get a basket." He wrenches a

blue, plastic hand-basket from the stack and starts down an aisle, but I can tell his mind is someplace else. The veins in his neck and arms are bulging. His muscles remain tense as I shadow him around the store, grabbing the basics—bread, eggs, milk.

The bell rings as the door opens. Dad startles again.

Wade marches toward us. "It's time," he whispers.

"Now?" Dad asks. "But I've got my kid here with me."

"What's going on?" I ask.

Dad shushes me.

Wade scowls, making his scar pucker along his cheek. "You made an oath, soldier. Have you forgotten?"

"No, sir," Dad says as he hands me our food basket.

Wade shoos me with his scarred hand. "The boy can finish your shopping."

Dad quickly passes me a couple of twenty-dollar bills from his wallet. "Go to the truck when you're done. Wait there. Understand?"

What's he about to do? I want to ask him what's going on. Instead, I swallow and nod.

Dad follows Wade like a loyal puppy; the bell rings as they exit.

Something's not right. I reach for my phone, but then realize I left it at the cabin. Not that I could probably even get it to work, since I couldn't get service last time we were here. Plus, now it has the newly added problem of a broken screen.

The heat of frustration creeps in on me, but I force myself to take a few deep breaths. My stomach growls with hunger.

Trying to take my mind off my shattered phone, I sweep the store for necessities: Pop-Tarts, Doritos, Dr Pepper, and, for protein, beef jerky. Finally, I pass the popcorn machine until I reach the glass case at the rear of the store. With one hand on the greasy handle, I reach under the heat lamp and grab a fried burrito by its paper sleeve. My mouth waters, but the clerk gives me the stink-eye, so I decide to eat while I wait for Dad in the truck.

After the clerk sacks our groceries, I step into the late-afternoon sun, scanning the horizon beyond the gas pumps. Even though it's almost five o'clock and even though we're in town, there's only the occasional passing car. A small blue truck sits hooked to the gas pump on the end while its driver cleans his bug-splattered windows.

I eye Dad's filthy truck. It would take a whole lot more than a sponge and a squeegee to clean this mess.

Where is he?

Dwight slumps in the back seat, his baseball cap pulled over his eyes. He's snoring with the gun I'd reassembled propped against his chest. So much for "keeping watch."

Moving to the other side of the truck, I open it and place my sacks on the floor in the back before grabbing my beef-and-bean burrito.

The soft whirr of an engine fan catches my attention. About a block away, an armored truck pulls up to GEO'S PIZZA & DONUT SHOP.

I take a bite through the flaky crust, savoring the salty beef and beans when, out of nowhere, two men with red bandannas covering the bottom halves of their faces race around the armored truck. One of them disappears behind the truck. Within seconds, the other drags the woman driver outside. She seems to be alone. I choke and cough as the man covers her mouth with his hand, bending the woman's arm behind her back. He snatches her gun from its holster and holds it against her head.

My heart races. I cough again, dropping my burrito. The meat and beans splat against the pavement. From out of nowhere, the man who disappeared reappears, carrying a black drawstring bag. I open my mouth to scream, but the words are stuck to the burrito glob inside my throat.

The man with the black bag taps the guy holding the woman as he passes him. That one shoves the woman to the ground, facedown, yelling, "Don't move!"

Then suddenly, they're running toward me, bandannas

sucked into their mouths with each breath. The man clench-
ing the bag is out front. I gasp, recognizing the run. Dad.

Somehow, they've changed clothes. Both are in black,
except for the red bandannas.

My heart skips a beat as I squint and spy the scars on the
other man's hand. Wade.

When they reach the convenience store parking lot, the
armored car driver screams for help.

"Get in!" Dad yells, and I realize he's talking to me.

My feet come unstuck as I dive into the back seat of the
truck, waking Dwight. He sits up with a start, pulling a
bandanna from his pocket to cover his face. He scrambles for
his gun.

There's movement coming from the direction of the
pumps and, through the back window, I see it's the guy with
the blue truck. He pulls a shovel from the bed of his truck
and runs after Wade.

"Shoot him!" Wade yells.

"What?" I shriek.

"Do something!" Dad yells.

"I'll do it." Dwight positions the gun I assembled in his
open window. I cover my ears as he pulls the trigger. Nothing.
He does it again. Nothing.

Dwight curses and screams, "The bullets!" He fishes in the seat pocket to retrieve them.

Dad's almost to the truck. The man from the pump is closing in.

"Get my gun!" Dad yells.

Suddenly, I remember the handgun he keeps under the front seat.

Dwight pushes my shoulder. "Help him!"

"How?" I ask, shaking my head. I'm not going to shoot someone. I can't.

Dad yanks open the passenger door and slides onto the seat, reaching. He plucks his gun from underneath and, with the door still open, points it at the guy.

"No!" I scream.

The guy immediately drops the shovel with a clang. He turns and runs toward his truck as Wade jumps into the driver's seat, and glances back at me. "Put your hood up," he orders.

Dwight jerks it over my head.

"What are you doing?" Wade asks. "Shoot him!"

The guy is getting in his truck; Wade turns the engine when Dad levels his gun.

My breath catches. *No, don't do it!*

The tires screech as Wade throws the truck in reverse, Dad's door swinging on its hinges.

A shot rings out. I jump a split second before the sound of exploding air. Another shot. Another explosion.

My heart's about to beat out of my chest. And then I see: Dad's blown the guy's tires. The front of his truck sinks to the ground.

"You missed!" Wade shouts as he tears from the parking lot. The smell of burning rubber fills my nose.

Dad stretches for the door handle and slams it shut. "I'm sorry, sir." But I know he didn't miss. He never misses. "What the hell was that, Rebel?" Dad shouts, the gun still in his hand.

I'm shaking. My head's shaking. My body's shaking.

The bag in his lap has come open. Money spills across the seat.

There's lots of it. Like lots and lots of money. Why would he do it?

They rip the bandannas from their faces as Wade speeds along the highway. He pulls a gun from his waistband. "Pirate booty," he says with a laugh, and I realize it must be the gun he took from the armored car driver. Wade waves it like a prize before tossing it onto the money on the seat.

But that doesn't make any sense. If he had her gun, why did he order Dad to shoot?

Wade looks to the money and then over at Dad with a slimy grin. In the rearview mirror, I can see the look of triumph in Wade's eyes. I shiver as he turns toward the mountain, gassing the engine. "Soldier, welcome to the Flag Bearers."

TWELVE

It's long past midnight; my arm tingles beneath the weight of my head. I shift under the thin blanket and follow the sliver of moonlight with my eyes, up the wall from the futon to the NEW WORLD ORDER sign with the red line running through it. I close my eyes again.

We're still here, living in the woods with the Flag Bearers. My dad's a thief.

After the robbery, he told me to take the groceries to the cabin, get something to eat, and go to sleep. That's it. No explanation. Nothing.

I tense up, hearing the thunk of footsteps on the porch. The cabin door swings open and, by the way he moves in the dark, I can tell it's Dad. I'm used to hearing him pace.

I keep my back to the cabin, not daring to turn over, not

knowing whether Angry Dad will be there to yell at me since I'm still awake.

There's a *click*. A light glows dimly behind me, and suddenly it sounds as if there's a large stream of water. I quietly turn over on the futon to my other side. Through barely open eyes, I spot Dad pouring a gallon-sized baggie full of sand across our table. He's too focused on what he's doing to notice me.

Then I spot the open liquor bottle in his hand. When the first bag is empty, Dad takes a long gulp. I curl my fingers against the thin mattress as he grabs another bag of sand and pours it across our table. He reaches into a box and retrieves a plastic soldier. I bite my lip, realizing what he's doing. Unable to watch, I immediately turn over and face the wall, praying for sleep.

***

The high-pitched chatter of birds awakens me. The room is dim except for the line of sunlight peeking between the black curtains near the front of the cabin. Dust motes float in the bright stream of light.

The sound of heavy breathing is coming from nearby. Dad is asleep, slumped in a chair next to the table. Last night's liquor bottle sits on the floor against the leg of his chair. It's been emptied by at least a third, and I definitely don't want to be the one to wake him.

I slowly roll off the futon, stiff from the thin, hard mattress, and stretch my arms overhead. A cardboard box marked in Dad's scratchy handwriting—REBEL CLOTHES— sits on the floor to my left beneath the REBEL COMICS crate. Quietly, I slide my comic books to the floor and open the box underneath, digging until I find a clean pair of jeans and a blue T-shirt from last summer's robotics camp, where Ajeet and I were both counselors for the younger kids. I hold the T-shirt to the light; a knot forms in my throat before I toss it inside the box and find a bright yellow one that doesn't remind me of what I'm missing.

Dressed, I slip toward Dad, stalling a second to make sure he's sound asleep. QUEN-10 and my shattered phone have disappeared from the table, replaced by a completed battle scene.

From what I can remember, it looks the same as the one in our basement at home. There are the same tanks, the same shooting soldiers. The road through the center of it all. The trucks in a line behind the tanks. The smoke coming from a ruined city. The dark-skinned men, sprawling and limp in the sand.

But there's something else, too. Something I've never

noticed until now: a girl. She wears a headscarf, waving on the side of the road. She's holding what looks like a white plastic grocery bag. Why would there be a girl in the middle of Dad's battle scene?

Dad snorts, startling me. I ease backward with my hands up. I hold my breath, noticing the two days of dark stubble across his cheeks. He snores again; his heavy breathing resumes. I exhale before tugging the blanket from my futon and then carefully cover him with it.

My stomach rumbles as I shuffle over to the refrigerator, snatching a Dr Pepper from the fridge. The can opens with a *pop,* making me jump. But Dad doesn't move.

With continuous gulps, I empty the can and hurry to close my mouth, holding in my massive belch, only to burn the lining of my nose when it finally comes.

I wipe my watery eyes; the chair creaks as Dad shifts and smacks his mouth. His eyelids are still closed, but it looks like he's waking. No time to find the box of Pop-Tarts, I snatch the closest thing—a few slices of white bread from the sack on the countertop. I shove them in the pocket of my hoodie and hurry outside.

The trees sway in the morning breeze, as if they're breathing in and out. I take a deep breath, too, and round the cabin.

"Rebel!" Dad screams.

My heart jumps. There's no way I'm stopping now.

Birds chirp as I slip-slide downhill and move fast downstream. The creek gurgles and splashes to my right. Suddenly, I realize I should've used the bathroom before I left.

To keep my mind off my full bladder, I tear pieces of bread and roll them into tiny balls before popping them inside my mouth. I wish I had some butter or jelly, but we didn't buy any.

"It's fine," I say to myself. I'll take a little walk and return after Dad's had a chance to eat some eggs. He's always better after he eats.

The thought of food makes my mouth water, but I shove another ball of bread between my lips to absorb the spit.

Before I know it, I'm at the waterfall. The pressure in my bladder is getting worse by the second; I know I can't ignore it much longer. I kneel in the leaves and check over the edge of the rocks, making sure that Calliope girl isn't there. That's just what I need—something else for her to laugh at me about.

There's a tiny rustle; I jump at the sound. But it's only a squirrel, skittering across a branch before jumping to another tree. I stand and, with one last check, relieve myself against a large boulder.

With the pressure gone, I descend the rocks, step-by-step, until I'm at the base of the waterfall where the creek flows into a calmer stream. I crouch and slip my fingers beneath the cool water. Tiny fish scatter in twenty directions. I shake my fingers above the surface and dry them against my hoodie.

My stomach growls. Even with the balls of bread in my stomach, I still feel empty. I think of Aunt Birdie's cooking: her chicken fried steak and peach cobbler. I shake my head. "No," I say aloud, stopping my train of thought.

I keep moving until I reach the fallen tree, the one Calliope used as a bridge. I put my foot on the gray log, testing it. The dry bark rasps against the sole of my shoe. With my arms out to my sides to keep balance, my left foot joins my right on top of the log. I sway a little but check myself before starting the slow sideways shuffle.

Midway across, I peer down. I'm a few feet above the water and catch my reflection: hair sticking out in all directions. Aunt Birdie would have never let me leave the house looking like this. I attempt to smooth my hair with my hand, but it's no use.

The leaves whisper and, from out of nowhere, the smell of something earthy and sweet draws my attention away from my reflection. My stomach rumbles again. The smell seems to be coming from beyond the trees. I shuffle a little farther and hop off the log, next to the place where Calliope stuck her fishing pole.

The delicious scent is stronger on this side of the creek. I hesitate, knowing I could get lost if I wander away from the stream. But the smell is so strong; it can't be far.

Inside the web of trees, twigs snap beneath my feet as I follow the sweet scent into the sunlight. On the edge of the tree line is a wide-open meadow, carpeted with clover and thousands of little white flowers. I bend over and take a whiff, but it's not exactly the same inviting smell.

Shading my eyes with my hand, I scan the horizon, where the mountains rise again past the meadow and notice a dark green shed to my left, along the edge of the field of flowers. The white blossoms gently sway in the breeze; the smell grows stronger.

Without thinking, I start across the valley, moving toward the shed, but stop mid-step when I hear bees buzzing nearby. They flit and hover from flower to flower. I give them a wide berth and continue to move across the meadow—toward the scent.

Without the cover of trees, the sun bakes the top of my head. Sweat slicks my forehead. I wipe it with the back of my hand and pull off my hoodie before tying it around my waist.

As I approach the green shed, I try to memorize where I've been and notice how the woods gradually slope upward, reaching for the sky. Cloud-shaped shadows crawl across the valley. It's so quiet here. I take a deep, sweet breath and smile.

The shed's wide planks are painted a dark green, matching some of the surrounding trees. I round the building and, on the other side, find another field of flowers—short red ones.

The delicious scent is so strong here, my mouth waters. On this side of the shed, there's a round sign with a sprawling bee in the center of the words: PASTOR WILKES' 100% PURE HONEY & JAM.

I lick my lips and notice the low humming sound coming from outside the shed, when I spot the stacks of pine boxes. I near them; the sound and smell are almost too much to bear.

Bees ignore me, buzzing and zipping from the flowery fields into the boxes and out again. Beehives.

Beneath one tower of boxes is a crate, full of mason jars. I pull one from the crate and hold the liquid gold up to the sunlight: honey.

Bees continue to move in and out of the boxes as I slowly

twist the brass ring and then pop the lid from the jar. I dip two fingers into the thick liquid and stick them inside my mouth: sweet, spicy heaven.

"What are you doing?" a high-pitched voice asks, startling me.

I drop the jar, oozing liquid heaven across the dirt.

Calliope is standing there with a handful of labels that look like the sign on the shed.

Bees buzz over the spill; my cheeks flush. Guilty, I bend to retrieve the jar.

"No, don't," she warns.

A sudden, sharp pain shoots through my arm; I cry out. On instinct, I slap. There's a bee stuck to my skin. It falls off, dead, floating in the pool of honey at my feet.

"What are you doing?" Calliope says again. "They release an alarm pheromone when you crush them."

I can hardly process what she's saying. My arm is throbbing and turning red. The bees are angrily buzzing. My heart hammers.

From out of nowhere, there's a shot of cool mist in the air, dampening my face and skin. "Move," she orders, pushing me aside. She's dropped her labels and is holding a spray bottle.

"Where did you get that?" I ask.

She doesn't answer as she releases another rapid shot of mist in the air. The humming softens a little.

My arm is swelling; I feel woozy.

"Are you allergic?" she asks.

I stumble a little, seeing the red welt on my arm.

Calliope shakes her head. She's looking at me like I'm a complete moron—which I've already figured out, thank you very much—and snags my hand. "Come on," she urges, gently pulling me away from the hives.

I'm too dizzy to protest—partially from the bee sting, partially because a girl other than Aunt Birdie is holding my hand.

She draws me through the field of red flowers; the soft petals bend as our shoes brush against them. Calliope's hair bounces as she moves.

I glance at my aching arm; it's swelling even more. I put my free hand on the place where the bee stung, and it's warm to the touch. That can't be good.

We soon reach the edge of the field, where there's a caramel-colored cabin. A heavy coat of lacquer makes the wood shine in the sunlight. On the right side of the roof, a tiny satellite dish angles toward the sky. Below the dish, a minivan sits on the short driveway next to the cabin.

"Where are we?" I ask as we clomp up one of the zigzagging ramps that leads to the front door.

Calliope drops my hand. "This is where I live," she says without stopping.

I grab the handle on the side of the ramp. "Your parents are going to kill me, aren't they?"

"Don't think so." A smile lifts the corner of her mouth. "I don't have any."

Huh?

"Come on," she says, gesturing for me to follow her as she opens the wide red front door of the cabin.

I don't move.

Calliope stops in the doorway, pointing to my arm. "Are you going to let me fix that for you or not?"

I think of how I treated her before: I was horrible. "Why are you being so nice to me?"

"No idea," she says and goes inside.

I shuffle the rest of the way up the ramp until I pass through the doorway into the living room.

The cabin smells of bacon and coffee. There's a blue plaid sofa and an overstuffed leather chair. One wall is covered with floor-to-ceiling bookshelves, full of all kinds of books, and a stone fireplace that looks dormant for the spring. From somewhere else in the cabin—it must be the television—a woman gives the daily weather report.

"Is that you, Peanut?" a man calls from the next room.

I stiffen. "I thought you said you didn't have any parents."

The TV voice suddenly stops.

Calliope shuts the front door. "I don't. Josiah—he's sort of my grandpa." I wonder what she means by that, but then she turns toward the direction of the voice. "We have company," she announces.

There's a rubber sound—like bike tires—rolling against the wood floors. Through the wide doorway emerges an older black man in a wheelchair. "Who do we have here?" he asks when he sees me.

I swallow hard. His legs have been amputated from the knees down. His gray pant legs are tied in large knots.

"This is Rebel," Calliope says.

The man offers his hand for me to shake.

I think of Dad and the Flag Bearers. What would they think of me being here? What would they say if they saw me shake this man's hand?

Josiah pushes his hand toward me and smiles. "Promise it's not contagious," he teases, eyeing his missing legs.

My face goes hot with embarrassment; I promptly take his

calloused hand and shake. "Rebel," my voice squeaks. "Rebel Mercer."

"Good to meet you," he says with a squeeze before releasing me. "Josiah Wilkes."

"*Pastor* Josiah Wilkes," Calliope adds, like she's proud.

Josiah smiles in response and rolls toward the fireplace. "True, true."

"He's the pastor of the AME Zion Church over in Mercy."

"AME?" I ask

"African. Methodist. Episcopal," Josiah answers. "So what brings you to our valley, Rebel Mercer?"

I clear my throat. "I, uh . . ." I shift between my feet. "I was following the sweet smell."

Calliope snorts a laugh.

"Enticing, isn't it?" Josiah says. "'Eat honey, my son, for it is good.' That's from Proverbs."

"And if we don't get the stinger out, it's going to get infected," Calliope adds.

I glance at my arm and, for the first time, spot the black stinger embedded under my skin. My stomach turns as I look away.

"I'm sorry," Josiah says. "That's strange. Usually they don't sting."

I hold my breath, expecting Calliope to rat me out for my

stupidity, but she shakes her head. "I'm going to get the first aid kit."

I try to breathe.

"Won't you sit?" Josiah asks.

"Thanks," I say, easing onto the cushy plaid sofa. Suddenly, my eyes feel heavy. If only the futon was this comfortable, maybe I'd sleep a little better. Or maybe if it weren't for the guns and war cries, maybe I would.

"You can ask me, you know?" Josiah says, and I realize I've been staring at his missing legs.

I shift, uneasy. It's probably rude to ask, but I am curious. "How did you—" I ask, pointing.

"Vietnam," he says matter-of-factly. "Land mine got me."

"You were in the Vietnam War?"

"Yes, sir. Joined for the GI bill. United States Marine Corps," he says with a firm nod. "Lance corporal."

"My dad's a Marine," I say. "Staff sergeant."

"Really?" Josiah sounds impressed.

I lift my chin a little.

"Active duty?"

My chin sinks. I don't want him to think any less of my dad for being on forced medical leave, so I nod.

"Bet your mom's happy to have him home."

I check over my shoulder. What's taking Calliope so long?

"She'll be a second," Josiah says.

"My mom died a little over a year ago," I admit under my breath.

"Oh." Josiah's voice falls. "I'm sorry to hear that. Really sorry."

By the way he's looking straight at me, I can tell he means it. Most people look away.

"You're enjoying a little vacation with your dad, then?"

I press my lips together and nod. Something like that.

He thumbs behind him. "You staying on the other side of the pass at the old Holloway campgrounds?"

I don't want to keep lying to him—he seems like a really nice man—but what choice do I have? It's not like I can tell him: *Oh, no, I'm staying at the camp full of racists who'd kill us both if they knew I was sitting in your living room.*

"Found it," Calliope says, saving me from another lie. She carries a white box with a red cross on it and a glass of fizzing water with a skinny potato in it.

"Here," she says, handing me the glass.

I turn up my nose. "Potato water?"

She laughs. "It's a stick of ginger, silly. It'll help with the nausea."

Josiah nods, gesturing for me to try.

I lift the glass to my nose and sip: spicy and refreshing. I drink a little more before she takes it from me, placing it on a corner table. She sits next to me on the sofa.

The hairs on my neck rise. I've never had a girl sit this close to me on purpose. She smells like honey and lemons.

Calliope places the box on the cushion next to her right hip and retrieves a small square packet before ripping it open.

I lightly cup my hand over the sore spot on my arm. "What's that?"

"It's to clean the area, so I can get the stinger out."

I shake my head, keeping the spot covered.

She lowers her fingers to her lap. "Fine, you want to have an arm full of puss, that's your choice."

Josiah lets out a short laugh, and I can't tell if he's laughing at her or me.

"Whatever, fine," I say, trying to sound less nervous than I really am. I stick out my arm. "Just make it quick."

She pulls a small pad from the packet and swipes it across the sore place on my arm. It's all I can do not to flinch. Then she takes a pair of tweezers from the kit and, while twisting her face in concentration, pulls the stinger from my arm in one swift motion.

"See?" she says, placing the black stinger on the small pad. "Now you can heal." She spreads a small dollop of ointment across the swelling spot before rifling through the Band-

Aids—robots, Barbies, Care Bears—until she finds a Star Wars one. Like the ones Mom stuck on me when I was little. Calliope removes the paper from the Band-Aid and covers my sting with R2-D2.

I feel better already. "Thank you," I say.

Calliope smiles and then shifts on the cushion. "Did you know the average person can withstand more than a thousand bee stings before they die?"

Correction: I *did* feel better.

"For a kid, it's about five hundred." She tilts her head. "Unless, of course, they're allergic."

"*Calliope,*" Josiah says. "I'm sure Rebel's not really interested in those statistics at the moment."

"Oh," she says, rubbing her hands on her jeans.

"I'm sorry we don't have a phone for you to call your dad," Josiah says. "I never had one installed."

"You don't have a phone?" I ask, surprised. "What if you need help or something?"

"I have Calliope. In a pinch, she can roll my chair into the van and drive me into town."

"You can drive?" I ask, totally impressed. I can barely ride a bike.

Calliope shrugs.

Josiah raises a finger. "In a pinch she can. But now that it's summer break, we're staying put more." He smiles. "Besides, someone from the congregation usually stops by every few days to visit us."

"I think you mean to check on us," Calliope corrects.

"Wow," I mumble to myself. I can only imagine how disconnected they must feel out here. "What about a cell phone?"

"Yeah, we've got those. But no service," Calliope says like she's just as annoyed about it as I am.

I nod in solidarity.

"If you like, I can drive you into town to call the campgrounds," Josiah offers.

"You drive, too?" I ask and then bite my lip, wondering if it's rude to ask.

"Of course," Josiah says with a laugh to his voice. "My van has been adapted with hand controls."

"It's actually pretty cool if you want to see how it works," Calliope adds.

I nod, curious about the mechanics of it all.

Josiah rolls backward. "I'm sure your dad is worried about you by now."

Dad? Dread twists my insides. I can only imagine his reaction when he sees me with Josiah and Calliope. I guarantee it's worse than a thousand bee stings.

I hop from the sofa.

"Are you okay?" Calliope asks.

"Maybe some other time." I stumble toward the door. "Thank you."

"Always running," she says. "You can stay, you know."

"It's nice to have someone her age visit," Josiah adds. "I think she gets a little lonely without her friends in the summer."

She shakes her head abruptly, like she's embarrassed.

"Thank you, but I can't today." My fingers wrap around the doorknob.

Calliope flips open the lock. "Did I say something wrong?" she whispers. "Sometimes I rattle off facts without thinking." Her eyes are deep brown. They gently probe and make me want to spill the real reason I'm leaving.

But I can't.

I wipe my hands on my jeans. "No," I answer, a little too loud. "I just have to go."

Josiah raises a hand. "You're welcome back anytime."

I really do want to stay. She smells so good. And they seem so nice. So *normal*.

And that's exactly why I have to go.

Before I can change my mind, I yank open the door and run toward the trees.

THIRTEEN

The last few days, I've mostly unpacked and explored the woods on my own while Dad plays soldier with his new friends. He hasn't asked me where I go on my walks. Dad hasn't realized I've been stung by a bee. He hasn't reminded me to take a shower or told me to brush my teeth. (I couldn't stand it anymore; I did both.) Dad hasn't talked about the new/old war scene on our kitchen table or explained why he thought it was a good idea to rob an armored car.

That's why I was surprised when he nudged me awake this morning, announcing we're going into a new town. I wanted to ask if he's afraid of getting caught after he broke the law, but then I spotted the new license plate on his truck and decided to keep my mouth shut.

It's only Dad and me inside his truck, speeding along the highway in the middle of a caravan of Flag Bearers. The trees cling to both sides of the road. The sky is overcast and gray; clouds race alongside us with the wind. Dad's truck is now spotless, except for the intermittent spit-drops against the windshield from the gathering rain clouds.

We zip through a patch of road, where the trees have been sheared by loggers, who have left giant scars on the earth around us. An orange timber truck roars past, the long bed of the truck covered with fresh-cut logs. Followed by another truck and another.

Out of habit, I tap my front jeans pocket, the place where my phone should be. But ever since the war scene appeared on our table, I haven't been able to find it. I take a deep breath and rapidly exhale, forcing myself to ask, "Have you seen my phone?"

Dad's jaw clenches for a second and then relaxes; he doesn't look at me. "Screen was broken. I got rid of it."

"What?" I screech, sitting up, nearly strangling myself with the seat belt. "Why?"

"You were too attached to it," he says, his voice gruff.

Seriously? "I'm a teenager. I'm supposed to be attached to my phone."

"They were using it to spy on us."

My fingers dig into the seat. "What are you talking about?"

Dad's knuckles turn white. "The New World Order."

Not *this* again.

We pass a giant WELCOME TO MERCY, OKLAHOMA, POPULATION 6950 marquee and take the first left, following Karl's black truck. Dad points. "Do you see the street signs?"

I glance at the neighborhood signs as we pass each block—Johnson Street, 1st Street, Washington Avenue—and nod. "So?"

"So," Dad says. "There's numbers on the backs of those signs."

I have no idea what he's talking about. What does that have to do with my phone?

"The New World Order put those there. FEMA has established numbered concentration camps on the East and West Coasts."

"Who?" I ask.

"The Federal Emergency Management Agency."

He's not making any sense. Aren't those the people who respond to natural disasters like the hurricanes in south Texas? "I thought they provided food and shelter and stuff."

"It's all a cover-up," Dad says as he makes another turn behind Karl.

A *cover-up*? He can't be serious. I open my mouth to tell him how crazy this all sounds.

Dad slows at a stop sign. His expression is tight, serious. Everything bulging.

Maybe another time. I press my lips closed.

"The numbers on the backs of the signs correspond to which camp the government is preparing to take people. Each neighborhood has a number." He gasses the engine.

I shake my head. "Who told you this?"

"What does it matter?" Dad asks. "It's the truth."

"But why would the government put people in concentration camps?"

"Because they want to eliminate the threat."

"What threat?"

Dad shakes his head. "Jeez, Rebel. For someone who's really smart, you sure ask a lot of dumb questions."

I flinch.

He speeds through a stop sign. "The New World Order has spies everywhere, trying to take us down." Our tires squeal with the next turn. "Where have you been going when you leave each day?"

Now he wants to know? I wasn't fishing with him, that's for sure. Even though that's exactly what I've wanted to do since we got here. "You've been busy."

He gives me a stern look.

I sigh. "I just go for walks, okay?"

"I don't think so." We pull into a parking lot and park in front of a beige metal canopy that covers a large concrete pad in the shape of a T. The longest part is about the length of three basketball courts. Beneath the canopy, people are setting up fruit stands, flower stands, and craft stands. The rectangular sign on the canopy signals we've arrived: MERCY FARMERS MARKET.

People are hanging out in the cars around us. I guess they're waiting for the market to open.

Dad throws the gearshift into park. "Were you meeting with the FBI?"

I laugh, but then realize he's not kidding.

"Wade says they've planted spies in the woods surrounding camp."

I shake my head. "Of course not."

"Then where did you get that?" he asks, pointing to my Star Wars Band-Aid.

I can't believe how ridiculous he sounds. Does he really think I got an R2-D2 Band-Aid from an FBI agent? I shift under his stare. "I met someone in the woods, okay?"

"Who? A *spy*?"

"No," I say louder than I mean to and shrug, lowering my voice. "Just a girl."

"A *girl*?" he asks, full of disbelief.

And for some reason, it stings almost more. Is it really that hard to believe I could meet a girl? My gaze falls to my arm. The Band-Aid is curling along the edges. I press it down.

He nudges my arm, barely missing the sore spot. "So what's this girl's name?" he asks, his tone a little lighter. His eyes are suddenly smiling.

Good grief. Okay, I was wrong. I don't know which is worse—accusing me of meeting spies or asking me about a girl.

He playfully nudges me again. This is getting more uncomfortable than the time Ajeet and I challenged each other in the second grade to a match of who could stuff more Legos up our noses. Answer: It was a draw. The third Lego sent me to the school nurse.

All of sudden, it feels like we're being watched. Wade and his daughter, Morgan, stare at us from the other side of the windshield. They're standing near our front bumper with their arms crossed.

"Dad," I say, pointing to them. "They're waiting."

He shakes his head. "We're not getting out of this truck until you tell me her name."

This is agony. "Calliope, okay?" I say, throwing open the door. "Now, can we not talk about this anymore?"

"Yeah." His smile widens. "Sure, Rebs. Conversation's over. No problem."

Something about how he says it makes me realize it's anything but over. Ugh. I jump from the truck; a raindrop hits my shoulder, then my cheek.

"Let's get under the cover before the storm comes," Wade orders.

"Yes, sir," Dad says and pulls a couple of boxes from the bed of his truck before following them.

Laughter and chitchat echo under the canopy. There's a loud clap of thunder—a few people squeal—right before the sky opens up. Heavy raindrops drum against the metal roof. People escape their cars and run for cover, bumping into me as they rush to different stands.

"Let's set up," Wade instructs as we reach a folding table. Dwight and Justin are already there. Seeing Justin next to Dwight, both with their overbites, I finally see the resemblance. Except Justin doesn't have all the body hair. Not yet, anyway. They're securing a Flag Bearers banner with the black sun and moon to the front of the table.

Dad drops the boxes there.

"What are we selling?" I ask.

Morgan rolls her eyes before ripping a small packet from

one of the boxes Dad carried. "MREs," she says, waving it before my eyes like I'm supposed to know what that is.

I look to Dad for help.

"Meals Ready to Eat," he says. "Created by the U.S. Military."

I pull a package from the box, reading the label: PASTA MARINA WITH VEGGIE MEAT CRUMBLES. My stomach turns. I think I'd rather starve. "Who eats this stuff?"

"Lots of people," Justin says, throwing a catalog at me.

I catch it against my chest, crumpling the pages. I flip through and discover all kinds of survival kits: freeze-dried food, drinking-water packets, glow sticks, whistles, blankets, and more. I drop it onto the table next to the Multigrain Snack Bread, fortified with calcium, iron, and other nutrients. My mouth twists in disgust. "Why would anybody *want* to eat this stuff?"

"It's what's inside our bug-out bags," Dad says. "Trust me, you'll want to eat it when the time comes."

Morgan nods in agreement. "The New World Order is going to shut off our food and water supply. And we'll be ready." She pulls a pamphlet from the other box. "Here," she says, pushing it at me. "Read and learn."

I eye the pamphlet. On the front, there's a picture of Wade and Dwight holding an American flag with Morgan and

Justin standing proudly in front of them. At the bottom is the tagline: *Who Watches the Watchmen?*

"Good picture, huh?" Justin says, picking at the acne on his chin.

I'm already opening the pamphlet, reading about how "no one's safe" and "white culture is under attack" and "gun control proves the feds intend to disarm Americans in preparation for a communist-style takeover by the New World Order."

I've read enough. I toss the pamphlet to Morgan as a woman with a baby propped on her hip approaches. "Thank you for getting the truth out," the woman says under the heavy patter of rain. Her baby flaps his arms and feet, babbling.

"You're welcome, ma'am," Wade says. "Would you like to take a look at our catalog?"

"My husband's out of work," she says, shaking her head. "Lost his job because a colored guy would do the same work for less."

Dad stiffens next to me.

I point at the fruit stands, ready to get away. "Can we—"

His face twists in annoyance. He pulls a twenty-dollar bill from his pocket and stuffs it inside my hand. "You go without me."

Wade and Dwight are nodding sympathetically toward the woman, while Morgan and Justin hand her the same pamphlet I tossed. The baby tries to grab it.

My insides squirm at the thought of him being exposed to that.

"What line of work was your husband in?" Dad asks, sounding like he's ready to do some recruiting for the Flag Bearers.

My neck tightens. "I'm going to look around," I say, frustrated. But, of course, Dad is too busy to notice.

I move down a few stands, ranting in my head and not paying attention when I accidentally knock into a metal bucket that's collecting rainwater from the leaky roof. A splat of water from the ceiling hits my face. Heat creeps into my hands. Frustrated, I kick the bucket, making it clatter against the concrete.

"Hey," a lady says, barely dodging it. "Watch it. You could hurt someone."

I spin away and stomp toward the crowd of shoppers moving along the center aisle. Several adults pull red wagons, full of little kids and the fruits and vegetables they've bought, reminding me they aren't all here to talk about government conspiracies.

I force myself to slow down and take a breath. And then another. One more deep breath before I push Dad's money inside my front pocket and turn to the right, weaving between the people and stands of clay pots, feathered dream catchers, and T-shirts. There's a black shirt on display with bold, Star Wars lettering: MAY THE MASS TIMES ACCELERATION BE WITH YOU. I snort a laugh; my shoulders relax a bit.

The rain slows as I continue to meander between the sellers. Birds flap across the market, roosting in the rust-colored rafters overhead.

At the end of the row, I spot a comic book stand with a banner—MICK'S VINTAGE COMICS & SUCH—hanging across the front table. An old guy with a long gray beard in a Willie Nelson T-shirt is manning the booth. Dad would call him a "hippie." It's probably Mick.

I can't resist: I pass the vinyl records and near the comics section.

"Can I help you find something?" Mick asks.

"Just looking," I say.

He gives me a genuine smile. "Have fun, kid." Then, he turns to talk to another customer about the weather.

The rain has slowed to a steady patter as my fingers walk across the tops of the comics, flipping them one by one. I stop when I spot one issued by Marvel in the 1980s: THE 'NAM. On the cover, there's a huddle of soldiers colored in a strange blue, apparently preparing for a helicopter rescue in the rain. I flip through the pages and spy the explosions and bloody bodies. It makes me think of Josiah's missing legs.

I immediately return it to the table, flipping past until I spot a Classic Star Wars comic. I smile. Han Solo is on the front cover, floating over the moon and fighting a bad guy.

"How's the arm?"

I look up from Han and find Calliope standing next to a stack of She-Hulk comics. She's wearing an apron with a honeybee logo.

My stomach takes a loop. "Uh." I swallow hard, trying to keep my voice steady. "Good, I think."

She fingers the edge of the She-Hulk stack. "Do you know who the first comic superheroine was?"

There's a shout in the distance. My shoulders tighten. The Flag Bearers aren't far from here. What would they do if they saw me talking to her?

"I'm waiting," she says, drumming her fingers on She-Hulk's forehead. "Of course, if you don't know—"

"You can't be serious," I say, her insult drawing my attention to her face.

She seems to be fighting a smile. "Well, do you?"

"Fantomah," I say. "Everybody knows that." I return the Star Wars comic to its place.

She nods approvingly. "Most people say Wonder Woman."

"Amateurs."

Calliope lets her smile take over as she raises a finger. "But can you list three of her superpowers?"

I rattle them off easily: "Transforming objects, flight, levitating things."

"Yeah," she says. "And when she uses her powers, her face turns—"

"Into a blue skull," we say together and then laugh.

She shrugs. "But somehow she manages to keep all that curly blond hair on top of her bony head."

Okay, now I'm totally impressed. "You collect comics?"

"No," she answers. "I like trivia. Josiah and I like to watch *Jeopardy!* in the afternoons when I get home from soccer practice." She points behind me. I crane my neck and, at the other end of a row of stands, spot the honeybee logo on a round sign that matches her apron. The same logo that was on their barn. Josiah is placing jars of honey in a paper bag for a customer.

"You play soccer?" I ask, turning to her, wondering why she's even talking to me. Not only is she smart and can drive, but she's also an athlete?

She nods. "You play something?"

"Only if you count video games." I shake my head. "Let's just say I'm not that coordinated."

She moves a little closer.

I can smell the lemons and honey; my heart thumps.

"You really should stop by the stand for a sample. We're handing them out right now." She shrugs. "Or, if you prefer, I can turn my head and you can try to steal some again."

My cheeks flush.

She's grinning from ear to ear, her smile brightening her whole face. And I'm so, *so* glad I actually brushed my teeth and showered today.

"Come on," she says, heading toward PASTOR WILKES' 100% PURE HONEY & JAM.

I can't help it: I follow.

The air is damp and heavy with the sweet smell of fresh-cut fruit and flowers. I pick up the pace, but stop short as Calliope moves behind their table. Josiah—all smiles—chats and offers samples to the crowd. His booming voice tells people the proceeds from today's sales will go to a college scholarship awarded to one member of the community by the AME Zion Church.

I can tell it's working because more people are pulling out their money and gathering around their stand.

Calliope rolls the top of a paper bag and hands it to a customer. She brushes a stray curl from her face before helping the next person in line. Watching her, I have this strange feeling in the pit of my stomach—not a bad feeling, just strange and fluttery.

After a few seconds, I realize she's too busy. She was only being nice. She didn't really want me to stop by.

I wipe my hands on my jeans—about to turn around—when she spies me over a customer's shoulder. "Rebel," she calls and holds out a small plastic cup with golden liquid inside. "For you," she says and places it on the table in front of her.

I grin like an idiot as she gestures for me to come closer.

My feet move mechanically toward her as she bags honey and a jar of strawberry jam. She hands it off to a customer, thanking him.

"This is the kind you like, right?" she asks.

I don't know what to say, so I swig the golden liquid. It coats my tongue and the back of my throat.

"Yeah, that's the one," she says, offering me the jar, just like the one I spilled.

"I can't take it."

She puts a hand on her hip. "No, but you can buy it."

"O-Oh," I stutter. "Right. Of course," I say, reaching for my money.

She turns to help another customer.

"Well, look what the cat dragged in," Josiah says with a smile in his voice. He rolls his wheelchair to the front of the table and offers his hand for me to shake.

There are all these people here, and he's stopping to shake my hand?

I don't hesitate; I leave my money on the table and ease around the crowd. "It's good to see you, sir."

A woman shuffles behind me to pay Calliope for two jars of Pastor Wilkes' blackberry jam.

"How's the arm?" he asks, pointing to my curling Band-Aid.

"Good," I say. "Your granddaughter did a good job."

"Do you want jam to go with your honey?" Calliope asks, holding up my money. "And maybe a box of Band-Aids so you can take off that skanky one?"

Josiah shakes his head. "She sure got you."

"Like you even have Band-Aids," I say.

"Ha!" she responds.

"You should not have said that, son," Josiah says under his breath.

Calliope bends over, disappearing behind the yellow table-cloth for a second as Josiah rolls around the table to take over helping the customers.

All of a sudden, she appears with ointment in one hand and a Band-Aid in the other.

"Told you," Josiah says, bagging a jar of honey.

I bite down a grin as she rounds the table.

"Are you *trying* to get an infection?" she asks me.

"Yes," I say, unable to contain my smile. "That's exactly what I'm trying to do."

"Well, you're on your way." She grabs my wrist, sending a jolt of electricity along my arm. "Let me see it."

She carefully removes R2-D2, exposing a little pink dot. It looks so tiny now, really not worth fussing over. But I'm not about to stop her if she wants to help me heal.

Calliope tosses R2-D2 in a nearby trash can, and with her head bent, her curls spring near my face. I breathe in her smell and watch her forehead wrinkle as she slathers ointment on the spot and then sticks a new Band-Aid on my arm.

"There," she says with a laugh.

I look down and spot the pink Barbie princess Band-Aid on my arm.

She laughs harder.

"Very funny," I say, but I'm laughing, too.

"Rebel!"

I snatch my arm from Calliope's grasp. *No, not him. Not now!* My heart leaps to my throat as Dad storms toward us.

FOURTEEN

As Dad nears, I can see the veins popping in his neck. Dwight isn't far behind.

My heart slams against my chest.

"What's going on here?" Dad shouts as he walks.

People turn to stare. Calliope's mouth drops open in disbelief.

No, don't embarrass me here. Not in front of *her*.

"Can I help you, sir?" Josiah asks, rolling to the front of the table, his chair creating a barrier in front of me.

"Get out of my way," Dad orders, and then looks across Josiah's wheelchair to Calliope. "What the hell do you think you're doing, touching my son?"

Her bottom lip trembles.

My whole body flushes with heat. My eyes feel like they're bulging out of my skull, willing him to stop.

"Sir," Josiah says, his voice a little louder but still calm, "I'm sure this is all a misunderstanding. Your son was contributing to the scholarship money my church is collecting."

"Your *church*?" Dwight says past the tobacco wad in his mouth.

"Yes, sir. I'm the pastor here at the AME Zion Church, and we're selling honey and jam to raise money for the community scholarship fund."

"Why was she touching you?" Dad snaps.

He makes it sound so dirty. I wish I could melt into the concrete floor and disappear.

"My granddaughter was putting a Band-Aid on your son's arm, sir. The other one was falling off."

"*This* is Calliope?" Dad says.

I squeeze my eyes shut, willing myself to awaken from this nightmare.

"That's right," she says. My eyelids snap open. She's lifting her chin, while Dad looks at her with so much hate.

"I think we got off on the wrong foot here," Josiah says, obviously trying to draw Dad's glare away from Calliope. "Of course, I don't have any feet anymore," he says with a nervous laugh. "Lost them in the war. Rebel tells me we have the same kind of background, you and I."

The vein in Dad's forehead throbs as he speaks through

gritted teeth. "How dare you! We are *nothing* alike."

I should probably say something. But my tongue feels too thick. The words won't come.

"You're not fit to lick the dirt from his boots," Dwight says before spitting—a brown, slimy mass—straight at Josiah.

I cringe as tobacco juice slides down Josiah's cheek and soils his crisp white collar.

Calliope tenses next to me. She edges toward Dwight, pointing. "How dare you."

But Josiah puts a hand at her waist, shaking his head, stopping her.

"Is there a problem?" a police officer asks. Apparently, someone called the police. Thank goodness.

"No, sir," Josiah says, wiping his face and neck with a handkerchief. "Just a little misunderstanding."

The cop looks suspiciously between Calliope and Josiah. He turns to Dwight. "Are you alright, sir?"

Calliope's hand clenches by her side.

The cop's badge glints under the lights. "Did you not get the right change or something?"

Why is he assuming Josiah and Calliope did something wrong? Calliope's staring at me, as if willing me to speak up for them, but I'm too shocked.

Dwight chews his tobacco and spits on the ground near

their table, splattering the yellow tablecloth with brown juice. "Naw, we're good."

The officer nods. "Then move along please."

"Yes, sir," Dwight says with a mock salute and starts walking.

But Dad's not moving. He's glaring at Josiah. "Stay away from my son."

"Sir," the cop says. "I said move along."

Dad clutches my upper arm and yanks. Pain shoots to my elbow as he drags me the opposite direction. His face is almost purple; he's huffing with every breath.

"Rebel," Calliope calls after me.

I glance over my shoulder as Dad hauls me away. The cop's already gone.

"You forgot." She's holding the bag of honey and jam I'd bought with Dad's money.

Dad squeezes my arm even harder. I yelp.

"I'll take care of this," Dwight says, his voice gruff as he storms toward their table.

"What's he going to do?" I ask, my tongue finally moving. "Leave her alone."

As soon as Dwight reaches her, he swats the bag from Calliope's hand, sending it flying. The glass shatters on impact. Dwight laughs, and I could swear he sounds exactly like Chewbacca. Honey saturates the bag, staining the paper and oozing onto the concrete.

From here, I can see the disappointment on Calliope's face.

I want to tell her I'm sorry; I don't think like they do. I want to tell her I wish they weren't like this. But I don't say any of those things.

Instead, I rip the Band-Aid from my arm, tossing it to the ground, and run. Just like always.

***

"You shouldn't have lied to me," Dad hisses. I squeeze the pistol grip on the gun I'm assembling. When we returned to camp, Wade ordered me to put together a new batch of assault weapons as punishment for making friends with "the Negroes."

I should have never come to this place. I thought I could help Dad get better, but now . . . I *hate* how they talk about Calliope and Josiah like they're dirty. I hate that I couldn't speak, or didn't speak, when I probably should have. I hate all of these guns. The sound that vibrates through my body, long after it's been fired. The blood and blank stare I can't forget. I shudder. I *hate* what guns can do.

But somehow, these parts make sense to me in all the mess.

Like Legos. There's an order to things. They fit together in a logical way. Unlike Dad and me.

Parts for at least one hundred guns have been delivered from at least a dozen different suppliers. I've matched and spread the parts in order down a long table. Dad and I are the only ones inside the large building where Dad took the oath.

Gunshots pop outside on the training grounds as I attach an empty magazine to the bottom of the gun I'm working on. I scoot farther along the table with Dad pacing behind me.

"I can't believe you did that," he says.

Maybe if I keep ignoring him, he'll give up and go play soldier with everyone else. When I reach the end of the table, I grab a sound suppressor.

"I asked you a direct question at the farmers market."

"You asked me her name," I correct, wanting to add, *not the color of her skin*. Instead, I screw the suppressor onto the end of the gun's muzzle and add, "I told you her name."

I lower the assembled weapon into a wooden crate on the floor and walk the length of the table, returning to the beginning, hoping he'll leave me alone.

No such luck. His footfalls are heavy behind me. "You embarrassed me."

I stop mid-step. I embarrassed him? What about me? "Why do you hate them so much?"

Sudden confusion creases Dad's forehead. "Who?"

"Black people. Brown people," I say, counting off on my fingers until I realize there are too many groups to count. "Basically anyone who's not like us."

"I don't hate them," he says.

I scoff. "In case you haven't noticed, these Flag Bearers are white supremacists, Dad. You're a part of that now."

"I'm not a white supremacist," he argues and then promptly adds, "I'm a white separatist. There's a difference."

I shake my head. He can't be serious.

"Let me ask you this: Why would you want to mix with them? They're stealing our jobs."

I release a heavy sigh, not wanting to hear it for the thousandth time, and stomp to the end of the table.

But Dad stays with me. "And the rest of them are living off the system; off of taxes I paid into that system to support their fifteen kids from five different dads."

I cringe as I think of Ajeet's parents: His dad's a doctor; his mom's a lawyer. Pastor Josiah is a preacher and business owner. Mrs. Fuentes is a school principal; her son works at NASA. They don't live off the system, or have fifteen kids. And so what if they did? I'm sure they all pay taxes, too.

"I don't like seeing our country being taken over," Dad continues. "And it's our government's fault." He presses a finger against the table, so hard his fingertip turns red. "Those traitors in Washington have forsaken America and her constitution, giving all the power to the New World Order."

He's not making any sense. How can I even respond? I snatch an upper receiver to begin a new gun.

Dad reaches for a lower receiver and offers it to me. "White people are under attack; nobody's paying attention but us. Who watches the watchmen?"

I guess he wants me to answer, *WE DO*, but I shake my head.

He returns the receiver to the table. "You're supposed to be on my side." There's another burst of gunfire outside, startling Dad.

I drop the partially assembled weapon on the table. "I didn't know there *were* sides until we got here."

All of a sudden, he slaps his hand against the table, making me jump, along with the parts. "When are you going to learn they're not like us?" His face tightens. "First that robot boy."

His name is Ajeet.

"And now, this, this . . ."

My eyes burn. "Calliope," I say. "Her name is Calliope." I'm hot and cold and sweating.

"Why can't you be friends with kids that are more like you?"

"Would it matter?" I say, shivering. "You hate me no matter what I do anyway."

Dad blinks, like he's surprised. "I don't hate you. Why would you think I hate you?"

"Because you're always mad at me."

"That's not true."

"Whatever," I say, staring past him, my vision blurring the longer I stare because I refuse to blink. If I blink, I'll start crying. And I can't do that, not in front of him.

After a second, his voice softens. "I'm not always mad at you."

I try to focus on the black gun parts, when there's a sudden *boom* outside.

Dad jumps at the sound and starts rocking back and forth between his feet, his whole body tight. I shift uncomfortably; he rocks for a few more seconds and then comes to an abrupt halt. His hands unclench with a sigh. "I wish I was more like Wade." There's a sudden pain in his eyes. "Or even that colored in the wheelchair."

"Josiah?" I ask, confused. I thought Dad hated him.

He swallows hard, his Adam's apple sliding up and down his rigid throat. "At least when your legs have been blown off or when half your body's been burned by a grenade, people can see you've been hurt. At least people know, or might give a little respect or have some sympathy for the things you've sacrificed to keep this country safe." He rubs a hand across his damp eyes. "At least they don't have to be embarrassed because they're weak."

"You're not weak," I say, surprised.

Dad scoffs, rubbing his red eyes even harder.

I never knew he felt weak. He seems so strong. And I hadn't thought of it before, but maybe people don't care as much about the things they can't see. I know I sometimes forget he's hurt. "Maybe we should go home," I suggest.

Dad sighs, his hand falling from his face. "We can't."

"Of course we can."

"You're not listening to me," Dad says, his voice tight. "If we abandon our unit, we'll be viewed a traitor and then they'll . . . I don't know." Dad shakes his head with an edge of warning.

"They'll what?" I ask, my pulse jumping. "What will they do?"

"I'd rather these guys not find out I have a sister, okay?"

I swallow hard, reading between the lines. Someone must've made a threat. If we go home, Aunt Birdie will be in danger. Suddenly, I'm glad she doesn't know where we are.

"Besides, I finally feel like I have a purpose again." Dad awkwardly smiles and nudges my arm.

Purpose? Are you kidding me? "You robbed an armored car. That's a crime, Dad." I shake my head. "Someone could've gotten hurt—or killed."

Dad wags his finger. "No one was hurt."

"This time," I say, my voice rising. "What if they catch you? What then? You could go to jail." I clutch my chest, dizzy. "*I* could go to jail."

"You're not going to jail."

"How do you know that? I was there. I've heard about those accessory things on TV."

"Rebs," Dad says softly. "I really, really need this. Please give it a chance. It'll get better." He lays a gentle hand on my shoulder. "Promise." His eyes don't waver.

"But you promised we'd go fishing, too, remember?"

Dad looks at me for a second, and then his expression changes. He barks a laugh, startling me, before his laugh turns deep and throaty. It's the first time I've heard him laugh—a real one—since we arrived.

"It'd be nice to do something normal for a change," I say, wanting to add: *Most kids don't go on camping trips with their dads for the weapons assembly and training.* But I keep my mouth shut about the last part.

"Yeah, okay," Dad says, still smiling. "We'll go fishing."

I'm about to ask when, but the screen door slams against the inside wall.

"Soldier," Wade barks from the open doorway, startling us both.

"Yes, sir," Dad answers, his body stiff, heels clicking together.

Wade marches inside, letting the door slam behind him. He follows the length of the table, inspecting my progress, before he points to the crate. "At least your boy can do something right."

"He'll be finished within the hour, sir, and ready for the next shipment."

The next shipment? How many guns do these people need?

Wade nods his approval. "Come help demonstrate a lateral advance for the kids."

"Yes, sir," Dad says, not even trying to hide the excitement in his voice.

"You'll need one of these." Wade pulls a fully assembled weapon from the crate.

Dad takes the gun and removes the magazine clip to check. Empty. He shoves his open hand at me. "Twenty rounds."

I press my lips together. I meant to leave the bullets packed in their boxes. These parts without the bullets are just a bunch of parts that click together like a robot. But once you add the bullets . . .

"Is there a problem?" Wade asks.

"N-no, sir," I mumble, shuffling over to the pile of cardboard boxes. Inside the top box, there are stacks of smaller green-and-white boxes labeled 223 REMINGTON/55 GRAIN. A shiver goes down my spine before I carefully lift a box and open the lid.

One by one, I count twenty bullets.

"We haven't got all day," Wade scolds.

My hands shake a little as I lay the bullets on the table.

"Hurry!"

I startle, dropping the ones in my hands, the brass clinking together as they land.

Dad wastes no time in snatching them, quickly stacking them side by side inside the rectangular magazine. When it's full, he slams it into the bottom of his weapon and retrieves the earplugs from his vest, slipping them inside his ears.

"You'll want to see this," Wade says to me.

I focus on the parts in front of me, hoping he'll let me stay inside, away from the loaded guns outside.

But Dad shoves another set of earplugs into my hand, letting me know it really isn't an option.

With a sigh, I push in the plugs; they expand and muffle the sound of gunfire as I step outside. Late-afternoon sunlight warms my face in the clearing. Kids line a temporary chain-link fence surrounding the training area.

"Hey," I say to Justin and Morgan.

Morgan turns up her nose and marches to the farthest spot away from me on the fence.

"What's with her?" I ask Justin.

"We aren't supposed to talk to you," he whispers.

I guess they heard about what happened at the farmers market.

On the other side of the fence, barrels and stacks of tires have been spread, leading to a plywood structure shaped like a house. Human-shaped targets are scattered throughout the simulation. Justin leans against the fence. "If I were you, I'd stay away from *them*."

"Who?" I ask.

"You know who," he says under his breath. "People around here are pretty slow to forget."

Is that a threat?

"We are a go," Karl announces as he exits the plywood house, wearing a bulletproof vest and a helmet. He stands at attention next to the house.

Wade's scar wrinkles with a smile. From inside the fence,

he nods at Karl. "Gunnery Sergeant Thompson has set up a new simulation for us today." Wade lowers a bolt-action rifle on top of one of the barrels farthest from the plywood house before he gestures toward Dad. "And Staff Sergeant Mercer has agreed to help me demonstrate a lateral advance upon a closely guarded building."

As Dad crosses inside the fence, there's a sudden wave of electricity in the air. Many of the kids wiggle with excitement.

"In this simulation, we are on a rescue mission."

"Who are we rescuing?" a small voice asks.

Some of the bigger kids shush the girl with a bow in her blond hair. She looks about six or seven.

"It's quite alright," Wade says as he moves along the chain-link fence, nearing the girl. He lowers his voice. "We're rescuing little kids like you from a work camp." My stomach twists as Wade returns to his announcer voice: "The New World Order has separated children from their families, forcing them into labor camps, but who watches the watchmen?"

"WE DO!" everyone yells.

Wade nods at the little girl. She smiles up at him, like she's placed all her trust in him. I feel sick as he paces along the fence line. "That's right. We are the *true* defenders of American liberty. The feds have forsaken our country, but we'll take it back. *We* are the ones under attack. *We* are the endangered species."

I cringe. By we, I now know he's talking about white people.

His face is bright red, except for his scar, which stays a silvery white. "We will defeat the New World Order or die trying!"

Everyone erupts in cheers. Everyone except for the grown men standing at attention. Everyone except for the soldiers and me.

When the noise settles, Karl jumps over the fence in a single motion, landing on our side.

Wade kneels in the dry leaves behind the barrel that acts as a table for his rifle. Dad positions himself to Wade's left.

"Ready!" Karl yells as he slips behind the kids until he's standing next to me.

I scoot a little closer to Justin as Karl looks down the line of children and places a finger over his lips, telling them to be quiet. And then he points forward.

Boom! Wade's rifle fires, blowing a hole through the farthest human-shaped target. The smell of ammonia, then gunpowder, fills my nose.

Dad surges forward to the next barrel and ducks. With a glance, he fires. *Boom!* Straight through the middle of the target's paper skull. He moves sideways and forward to the stack of tires. Firing again. *Boom, boom!* Same result. Head. Heart. Again, advancing and firing with single-shot accuracy.

Over and over Dad makes the hit until he reaches the house, when, out of nowhere, Dwight charges from behind wearing the same bullet-proof gear as Karl. Dad's not wearing any protective gear. The bullets are real.

My hands clench the top of the sharp fence as Dad and Dwight wrestle with the gun. My heart races. Somebody could get shot. All the kids are cheering, but they could get shot. Dwight snatches the gun from Dad's hands. I gasp.

Dad sweeps his leg backward; Dwight drops to the ground. He grunts, his shaggy hair matted against his face. I manage a breath as Dad presses his foot into Dwight's shoulder, stealing back his gun. Justin shifts uncomfortably. Dwight squirms and roars until Dad presses the muzzle of his AR-15 into Dwight's lower back. Justin turns away from the fence, like he can't watch.

With his rifle pointed at Dwight, Dad snags the handgun from its holster and throws the plywood door wide open, revealing the life-sized pictures of children lining the walls inside the house. Many of them are pictures of the kids standing along this fence.

"Oo-rah!" Karl shouts over my shoulder, making me jump.

Wade stands from his hiding place, signaling the end of the drill. Dad returns his handgun to its holster and offers Dwight a hand up from the ground. The other kids clap as Dad gives Dwight a friendly slap on the shoulder. I clap, too, grateful Dad wasn't shot.

Dad grins when he sees me clapping for him.

It's hard not to get caught up in the fake children's rescue. We all cheer until I see Dwight push past Dad and spin toward the house. There's another *boom*, followed by silence. Dwight lowers the handgun he'd hidden in his belt; the other kids' shouts grow louder.

But I don't join them.

Chills run down my spine as I stare at the one shot Dwight made inside the house—the mangled photo of a child who doesn't look like the rest.

Justin sneers. "Looks like my dad just killed your girlfriend."

FIFTEEN

It's been a couple of weeks since I've seen Calliope. I wanted to find her sooner but didn't think it would be safe for her, or for me. They've been watching too closely.

But now some of the Flag Bearers have returned to the farmers market to sell survival kits. The rest are running drills, and there are not enough men to split watch between the camp and me.

Besides, I finally put on their uniform—black T-shirt, camouflage pants, and these awful black boots. Dad's been nagging me about it for over a week, and I finally gave in, hoping they wouldn't watch me so close if I looked like one of them.

Dad left before sunrise, and I'm now crossing the creek, scooting my new black boots sideways along the fallen log.

They pinch and rub my ankles, making me wish I had my old, dirty running shoes.

The shiny boots remind me of him, and I can't help but remember what Dad said: He thinks nobody cares he's been hurt. But I do.

And I don't want to hurt him more, which is why I still haven't asked about the one shot. Dad had rescued the children—every single one of them—but Dwight wouldn't let that happen.

And the cheers afterward? And what Justin said?

I mean, the picture with the hole through the face wasn't really a picture of Calliope, and she's definitely *not* my girl-friend. But it was a picture of a black girl and Calliope is my friend, or she was before I screwed things up.

Landing on the other side of the stream, my hefty boots squish the dew-covered leaves. I try to breathe in the smell of the coming rain, but it feels like I have a giant weight pressing on my chest.

As I clear the trees and slip into the meadow of white flowers, I spy the gathering clouds over the mountains—dark and menacing. It's like they're warning me to stay away, but I push forward anyway, moving through the flowers.

The sweet honey smell grows stronger as I round Josiah's shed and hear the low buzz of bees. I walk past the hives, giving them a wide berth so I don't get stung again. But there aren't any bees outside the hives today. It's as if they know a storm is coming.

Between the field of red flowers and their cabin, I spy Calliope running back and forth. My breath catches. She seems to be playing a game with herself. She's all laughter and smiles.

As I move closer, I can see she's dribbling a soccer ball the length of the lawn in front of her house. She looks so happy and free. I wonder if she feels that way inside.

I move through the red flowers slowly, releasing their spicy scent. Calliope kicks the ball between a pair of cones. It crosses an invisible line between them; she pumps her arm in celebration.

But as she turns, her face changes from a smile to a scowl. She's spotted me, and suddenly I wish I hadn't come and ruined whatever she was feeling.

Calliope immediately leans over and grabs her soccer ball, rolling it up the side of her long leg until it reaches the crook of her waist. She holds it there and spins away from me, hurrying toward the cabin.

"Wait," I call, waving a hand over my head like an idiot.

Of course, she doesn't stop. Why should she? Still, I'm running—or more like lumbering in these heavy boots—after her. Flower stems crunch beneath their weight.

"Calliope, I'm sorry," I say, already out of breath when I reach the ramps.

She's on the porch, next to the front door. She drops her ball on the rocking chair and turns toward the railing, looking down on me. Her eyes narrow. "I'll say this slowly so you can understand. Go—"

"I know you're mad," I say, cutting her off before she can tell me to leave.

She wipes the sweat from her upper lip. "Gee, how'd you figure that one out?"

"And I know I deserve it," I continue. "I didn't know what to do at the farmers market. It all happened so fast."

She crosses her arms over her body like a shield. "You lied to us. You said you were on vacation with your dad."

"I know," I say, my gaze falling to my boots.

"Why didn't you tell me you were one of *them*?" she says, practically spitting the last word.

"But I'm not," I say, vigorously shaking my head.

"Yeah, right."

I realize how I must look to her. I *do* look like one of them. "It's just my dad—"

Calliope puts a hand out, stopping me. "I have better things to do than talk to a lying racist."

Her words sting. A lot. "I'm not."

Her hand's on the door; she's leaving. I haven't said anything I need to say, and she's leaving.

"I'll beat you at your own game," I blurt. I don't know why I say it. It's like my tongue has been possessed, like I'm being controlled by some kind of Jedi mind trick.

"What did you say?" she asks, facing me.

Is *she* the Jedi? All I know is I don't want her to leave.

I point to the ball she's dropped in the rocking chair and clear my throat, trying to sound confident. "I'll beat you at soccer." My heart is beating fast. I can't play. She knows I can't play. But at least this is stalling her, keeping her on the porch a few seconds longer.

She picks up the ball and spins it between her hands, as if she's actually considering it. "And what do I get when I win?" she asks. The wood creaks as she descends the ramps.

I manage to breathe. She's not leaving. Not yet, anyway.

"What do you want?" I ask, my gaze following her until she's standing directly in front of me. "Name it. Anything."

Her hairline is damp with sweat. Her face all business. "For you to never come here again."

"Forget it." I shake my head.

She spins toward the cabin.

"Okay, fine," I say, reaching, wanting to touch her, not daring to touch her.

Calliope glares at me. "I'm serious." She's not smiling; I know she's not lying.

"Fine," I say again, desperate to keep her from leaving. Desperate to make things right. I want to go back to her rattling off trivia. Laughing at me; with me. And me pretending not to like everything about her.

She chews her lip.

"So what do I get if I win?" I ask, hoping to make her smile.

Calliope tosses the ball against my chest, knocking the air out of me. "You won't." She doesn't smile or take her eyes off the ball in my hands. "Between the cones is a score," she says pointing to the orange set on each end of the lawn. "First person to get to three goals wins, and I'll finally be rid of you." Her confidence is scary and appealing. "Oh, did I mention I've been playing club soccer for five years?"

"Great," I say and drop the ball on the dewy lawn.

She hops between her feet like an agile boxer and nods my direction. "I'm going that way," she says as I move away from the ball.

I swallow hard, trying to spread my feet like she has. But,

with the weighty boots, I'm even more awkward than usual. I can see the laughter in her eyes. Bottom line: She's going to kick my butt.

"Go!" she shouts, zigging to my left. I jump left to block her, but she's already zagging to my right. I hear the *thump* of impact and turn, only to see the ball fly easily between the cones.

Calliope jogs to retrieve the ball, her hair bouncing as she moves. In one nimble motion, she shovels the ball with the toe of her shoe and balances it on top of her foot. She kicks the ball in the air before catching it with both hands.

She really *is* good. Of course she is.

Calliope returns to center, dropping it in the lawn, and rubs her hands together with a *swish, swish.* "That's one," she says holding up her index finger.

"What's the bet?" Josiah yells. He's rolling along the front porch, eyeing me. It's the first time I've seen him since he was wiping Dwight's spit from his face. I want to shrink and disappear. But I force myself to stay put, shifting between my feet, expecting him to order me to leave.

"The first to three goals wins," Calliope answers.

"Who's winning?"

She grins, showing off her perfect smile.

"Alright, alright," Josiah says, "I get the picture." He rolls his chair closer to the railing, like he's trying to get a better view of my imminent slaughter. "Rebel, I think you might be in over your head here."

He's still talking to me? "Yes, sir," I answer and shove the sleeves on my black T-shirt to my elbows and crouch with my hands on my knees, trying to get ready.

Calliope straightens and taps a foot on the soft grass. "What are you doing?"

All of a sudden, I'm self-conscious squatting in front of her.

"This isn't wrestling, you know."

My face flushes with embarrassment, but then I notice the unprotected ball. "Go," I blurt and push off on my right foot, hoping to catch her off guard. Too bad I'm me.

My left foot slips on the damp grass; my arms flail but I'm on the ground, landing hard on my back, before I can stop her.

There's the *thump* again, followed by another score.

"That's two," she says like I can't count that high.

I sit, my hands and boots pressing into the ground in frustration. Pieces of grass stick to my hands. My backside is wet from the dew. Heat flickers across my skin.

She returns to center with the ball as I stand and brush the grass from my pants. She's not even breathing hard.

"Come on, Rebel!" Josiah yells from the porch. He's cupping his hands around his mouth. "You're letting her win!"

Letting her? I wipe my forehead on the shoulder of my T-shirt and try to stay calm. I take a deep breath and exhale. One more score and I'm finished. One more and I never get to see her again. I can't let that happen. "I'm sorry," I say. "I didn't mean to—"

"Oh, no. You can't back out now," she says, cutting me off. "A bet's a bet."

I shake my head. I take another breath. She thinks I'm talking about the soccer game. Why is this so hard? "That's not what I mean."

Calliope puts her foot on top of the ball, like she's ready to sink the final goal and get rid of me for good.

"I'm not like them," I say.

Calliope's jaw tightens. She draws the ball backward with the sole of her shoe, and then she punts. Hard, as if she's imagining it's my face. It sails between the cones.

"Game over," she says, gruff, before rushing toward the cabin.

Leaving me alone.

SIXTEEN

Game over? "Hey," I call after her. "I wasn't ready." Why wasn't I ready?

Calliope is already stomping up the ramps.

"That last one doesn't count," I argue, hoping Josiah will help me.

He says nothing; she's almost to the porch.

I follow her, trying to catch up. "Please," I say. "I didn't know they would do that."

She's not even giving me a chance to explain.

My hands clench from the unfairness. "What was I supposed to do, huh?"

Calliope stops mid-ramp. She spins around, her arms crossed. "If you have to ask, you're even dumber than you look."

I flinch.

"Calliope," Josiah finally speaks and then shakes his head.

"What?" she asks, her arms hugging her body.

"'Let every person be quick to hear, slow to speak, slow to anger.'"

She rolls her eyes. "Are you really going to quote the Bible to me now?"

Slow to anger? I take a couple of deep breaths and feel the heat escaping.

"You should hear the boy out," Josiah says, touching her elbow as she reaches the porch. "He did come all the way over here."

She rolls her eyes again.

"Thank you," I say as I join them on the porch.

"And then, if you're still unhappy with what he has to say, you can throw him out like yesterday's trash." He turns to me with one eyebrow raised.

Thanks a lot.

Calliope huffs and drops into the rocking chair. It creaks as she moves—back and forth, back and forth. "Fine, I'm listening," she says, without looking at me, glaring straight ahead.

Josiah gestures, encouraging me to talk. My tongue is dry. I wipe my hands on my pants and suddenly feel self-conscious. My fingers come away from my legs as I realize I'm staring at the knots in Josiah's pants.

Calliope clears her throat with impatience.

"I—I didn't know," I sputter. "I mean, I knew." This is why I don't speak.

Calliope stops rocking. She grinds the toe of her shoe into the porch, like she's had enough.

"I came here with my dad," I admit. "He wanted to get away from stuff." I swallow hard, choosing not to confess I wanted to get away from stuff, too. "I thought I could help him. But he joined this group."

"The Flag Bearers?" Josiah asks.

I nod. "Everything's so messed up." I turn to him. "I'm so sorry Dwight did that to you—spit on you, I mean—and that my dad said those things."

Josiah shakes his head. "It's not your apology to make, son."

"Why are you being so nice to me?"

"Because he's a man of God," Calliope answers. "Me, on the other hand . . ." She gives her head an abrupt shake and returns to rocking, her jaw clenched.

There's a low rumble of thunder in the distance; the quiet

on the porch is almost unbearable. I don't know where to begin. What are the right words? How do you say what's been pulsing in your mind for weeks? Years? I wish she'd save me and rattle off trivia or that Josiah would quote scripture again.

"War messes with a man's head," Josiah says instead, surprising me.

"What do you mean?"

Josiah gazes across the field of red flowers, almost like he's in a daze. "You leave as one person and come back as another."

It's hard to imagine him as anything but what he is: kind.

Calliope slides forward in her chair. "Were you different before the war?"

"Sure was," he says. "And when I came home, my life didn't quite fit together the same as it used to. Everyone had moved on with their lives, while mine had been forever changed." Josiah stares at his legs. "It was too much for me. I knew I had to get away from everyone." Suddenly, he winks at Calliope. "Except for your grandmother, of course. She knew how badly I needed this, so she abandoned the comforts of living in town to move to this empty valley with me." He laughs to himself. "Here she was such a fine southern lady. She loved to entertain—Sunday dinners, Wednesday-night Bible studies. And she gave those things up for me." He points. "I'm guessing like Rebel is doing for his dad now."

My cheeks warm. He makes it sound so noble, which I'm definitely not.

Josiah shrugs. "I suppose, deep down, I knew I needed the space to clear my head."

"My dad says he needs that, too."

"It's not uncommon with guys who've seen battle." Josiah crosses his hands over his lap. "But eventually, things started to make a little more sense. Breathing became easier." A smile brightens his face as he gestures toward the meadow. "I found God in this valley. My faith, along with some group counseling, helped me through."

I shift, uncomfortable. Josiah found God out here; Dad found the Flag Bearers. "My dad won't go to counseling," I admit, feeling an instant mixture of relief and shame for saying it out loud.

Josiah nods like he understands. "It's a struggle many veterans face. We're told we should be happy to be alive. People think we should be grateful to be back home. And we are, but that attitude also leaves folks feeling ashamed, scared, or too angry to ask for help."

Calliope tilts her head. "But that doesn't excuse ignorance, does it?"

"No, it doesn't," Josiah agrees. "But it can explain why Rebel's dad feels like he still has to fight an enemy, even if it's one of his own making." Josiah turns to me and points the direction of his shed. "Your dad's like that bee from the other day."

I shake my head, not understanding.

"The one that stung Rebel?" Calliope asks.

"Precisely," Josiah says.

I look between them, confused. "My dad's like—a honeybee?"

"Oh, I get it," she says, sitting up in her chair. "Did you know a honeybee dies after it stings someone?"

I'm relieved she's spouting trivia again, but I still don't understand what they're saying. It's like they're tossing out puzzle pieces without showing me the picture on the box.

"And remember how I said you didn't need to slap it?" she adds.

"O-kay."

"Your dad is like that bee." She puts a finger to the side of her head. "He only *thinks* he's defending himself. But he's not."

"He's not," I say, still not fitting everything together.

Josiah shakes his head. "He's on a path of self-destruction."

And suddenly, it's like he's flipped the last puzzle piece. Everything fits. Dad only thinks he's protecting himself. "He's been so busy defending himself, he doesn't realize he's actually hurting himself."

Josiah nods somberly. "When fear is at the center of your life, it's impossible to be your best self."

Calliope points to me. "Can I ask you something?"

I immediately nod.

"Do you think you're better than me?"

"Of course not," I say, thumbing toward the lawn. "I think you just proved that."

Calliope smiles, but it quickly fades. "You know that's not what I mean. You can't just stand there when people act like that. Like we're not even people."

I know she's right. "But what was I supposed to do? They're grown men. Not to mention the fact they have guns."

"Shouldn't you be used to the guns by now?"

"No." I shake my head vigorously and then wonder, turning toward Josiah. "Do *you* own a gun?" I hold my breath for the answer.

"Don't believe in them."

I exhale. "I hate them," I admit softly.

Josiah rolls a little closer, looking like he's figured something out about me, too.

My pulse jumps. He's going to ask me why I hate them. My hands are sweaty.

"You know, sometimes, if we talk about things, it's easier to let them go."

I reach back, clutching the poles of the porch railing.

Josiah shrugs. "Your choice."

"It doesn't matter."

"Seems to me it does," Calliope says.

"It's nothing. It was a long time ago." My hands slip from the railing. "Dad took me on a hunting trip when I was about eight, maybe nine, that's all."

"That's about how old I was the first time," Josiah says, his tone nudging.

"It was cold." I shiver from the memory of how cold it was. "We saw her breath before we saw the moose." I can still hear her gentle snorting sounds. "We were hiding inside of a deer blind when she came up to the feeder."

"Had you ever shot a gun before?" Josiah asks.

"Not really," I answer. "I guess Dad had shown me how to fire the rifle before then, but I really don't remember." My stomach turns. "I just know he told me to shoot."

"So you missed," Calliope says, gripping the arms of her rocking chair.

"There was a loud *boom*, but I didn't kill her." I hit her in the chest; it went through her back. She kept stumbling around for what seemed like forever. "Blood was everywhere." My heart thumps fast. Red was on the ground. On the leaves. She was making these horrible sounds. "I dropped the rifle. Dad yelled at me."

The gun had changed me, gave me a power I shouldn't have. I was crying. I guess I hadn't thought it through. Hunting sounded like something cool you did with your dad, but I didn't know what it meant. "It was cruel to leave her like that," I say.

But I couldn't shoot her again. I couldn't put her out of her misery. "Dad finished her." From then on, I refused to go hunting with him. It made him angry—*really* angry—but I saw what a gun could do.

"Sometimes, things aren't as easy as we think," Josiah reasons.

I bite the inside of my cheek and wipe my eyes.

"So what? You don't like guns," Calliope says, pointing the direction of the Flag Bearers' camp. "You must agree with them if you stay there."

The heat is instant. "I already told you."

"Did you?" she asks. "That's your problem."

The heat spreads to my face. "What? *What's* my problem?" I ask harshly.

"You don't ever say what you're thinking," she says, even louder. "Not really."

My breath huffs in disagreement, even though I know she's telling the truth.

"If you think he's wrong, you should tell him."

I tense another notch.

"Complacency is the same as affirmation," Josiah adds calmly.

Calliope gestures toward him. "He's right, you know. If you don't speak up, you might as well agree with him."

"But I'm just me," I argue. "I don't agree, but I'm not any good at that stuff. I never know what to say. Obviously."

Josiah presses his hands together, as if in prayer. "The Psalms tell us: 'God ordains strength out of the mouths of babes.'" He nods at me. "The voices of children matter, especially since they are often the only carriers of truth."

"But *how* do I tell him?"

"In your own words," Josiah says, like that helps.

"Do you like acting like a soldier?" Calliope asks.

Thunder sounds in the distance; I shake. "I hate it," I admit, which is the easiest thing I've confessed so far.

Her face softens. "Then tell him."

"How?"

"In your own way."

My own way. I glance at my black boots and camo pants. This is not me. But how can I tell Dad without hurting him?

Josiah rolls toward the door. "Since it seems the bulls have finally come out of the china shop, I should probably get back to preparing tomorrow's sermon."

Calliope springs from her chair. It rocks on its own as she opens the door for him.

"Pastor Josiah," I say.

He stops in the doorway

"I really am sorry about what happened at the farmers market."

"I know, son," he says with a nod and then closes the door, leaving Calliope and me on the porch.

There's an awkward silence, followed by the sound of thunder. Lightning flashes over the meadow. "You better go," she says, her voice flat.

My heart sinks, but I still dare to ask, "Can I see you again?" I'm afraid to ask and afraid not to. She did win the bet.

Calliope crosses her arms. "I think that depends on you."

At least it's not a *no*. My shoulders lift. I know what I have to do.

SEVENTEEN

Thunder claps; the trees around our cabin shake. My heavy boots thump against the porch as I breathe in the thick air of the coming storm and step inside.

Dad's snores roll from the upstairs loft. I breathe again. Calliope says I have to talk to him in my own way. His snores are long and deep. Looks like I have a little more time to figure out how.

I approach our table, taking in Dad's war scene. The sand, the soldiers, the smoke, and the girl waving on the side of the road. Why is she there?

The rain starts outside, pattering millions of leaves. I examine the table for clues. The line of trucks on the road. Soldiers running from a building with cottony smoke. And then I spot the new addition—the gun trained on the girl.

The soldier standing on the passenger seat of the Jeep, aiming his weapon right at her.

I shiver and back away from the table, tapping my pocket out of nervous habit.

But my phone's not there. I know Dad said he tossed it, but maybe he's actually hidden it. If it still works, maybe I can find a place with service and call Aunt Birdie.

While Dad snores, I quietly check the drawers of the kitchen, but there's only silverware in one and a Sharpie, a pencil, and a mousetrap in another. I move to the remaining boxes Dad had ordered me not to unpack and check over my shoulder.

He's still asleep upstairs, so I gently pull the tape from the nearest box. It's filled with rectangular things wrapped in newspapers—picture frames. I lift one from the box and pull off the wrapping. Mom's picture is right on top.

It's the one where she's laughing at Cadillac Ranch. I smile. It's like looking in the mirror—pale skin and tiny freckles on her cheeks. The only difference? Her eyes. Mine are green like Dad's.

It's almost as if she's staring right at me. It's like she's taken one look at the clothes I'm wearing and sees right through me. If she were here, she'd tell me to be myself. That's what she always told me to do, even though sometimes it's hard.

She told me I should show people who I am, even Dad. I thought it would be easier to pretend. But pretending doesn't seem to work—not really—especially since we've been here.

Maybe Calliope is right: Maybe it's time to tell him the truth.

Quietly, I remove the box of pictures from the top of the stack to get to the crates underneath. I find the one holding the pieces of QUEN-10 and the other crate holding my spare parts. Since the table is covered by Dad's war scene, I move to the kitchen with my supplies.

I take a chair from the table and sit, pulling myself as close to the countertop as I can. Gently, I disassemble the remaining parts of QUEN-10, laying them along the surface and then grabbing new ones from the crate: an EV3 brick, wires, color sensors, and the parts to make dog gears. My hand shuffles the pieces, tapping them as I assemble and rearrange them in my mind.

For the first time in weeks, a buzz of excitement runs through me. *This* is who I am. I'll build something better than ever before and show Dad, and he'll finally understand why we can't stay.

I open the drawer to retrieve the Sharpie and tear a flap from the cardboard box of pictures. I sketch a rough blueprint in red ink on the cardboard, careful to keep my marker from squeaking and waking Dad. I don't want him to see it until I've finished.

After I have my robot mapped out, I write his name at the top of the sketch, underlining it three times. I cradle his rectangular brain in the palm of my hand and set to work on N8TE.

***

"Wake up!" someone yells. A rough hand shakes me awake.

Bleary, I struggle to lift my face from the counter. N8TE is still charging, his red light flashing on the kitchen countertop. It took me all afternoon, plus seven Pop-Tarts, to finish him.

"I said *up*." Dad looms over me, holding an AR-15.

My heart skips a beat; I rub my eyes. "What time is it?"

"They're coming," he says. His gaze nervously darts around the cabin before he runs to flip off the light. The cabin goes gray.

"Who is?" I ask, adrenaline surging through my veins. Maybe the police figured out he was part of the robbery.

Dad ducks under the windowsill and carefully grips the corner of the black fabric, pulling away the curtain. He scans the woods. It's almost dark outside, but I can still hear the steady patter of rain against the leaves.

He glances at me, whispering, "Jenny, you have to hide."

Jenny? As in my mom?

"Get Rebel and hide under the bed," Dad instructs.

I bite my lip; my eyes sting. Does he really think I'm Mom?

"What are you waiting for?" he yells. "They'll be here any minute."

"Dad," I say, trying to keep my voice steady so I don't startle him. "It's me."

I sense the change in his body before I see it. He charges toward me, grabbing my shirt collar. "Soldier, what are you doing here?" Veins throb along his neck. "You never leave your post." He tosses me against the front door; my hands smack the wood. Pain shoots into my wrists.

His footsteps are fast behind me. I gasp as he grips the back of my neck, yanking me sideways, my head swinging like a rag doll's. He opens the door. "Go!" he screams, pointing at the woods.

My head throbs. I don't know where I'm supposed to go. Or what he wants me to do.

His body grows tighter and tighter the longer I don't move. "That's a direct order."

"Dad, please," I say again.

He grips my upper arm with one hand and pushes between my shoulder blades with the other; my feet shuffle against their will across the porch to the edge of the steps. The toes of my boots teeter over the edge, about to fall. He yells into my ear, "Soldier, I'm warning you!"

It's all I can do not to flinch.

"Stand post, now!"

I don't know what else to do; I stumble down the stairs and into the rain. My hair washes into my eyes.

He follows close behind, large drops streaming along his angular face. "Stand guard," he commands and shoves his weapon against my chest.

I fold in half from the impact and then force myself upright. Fearful I'll drop his gun, my fingers cramp.

In one motion, he jumps onto the porch and storms inside, slamming the door behind him.

Thunder rumbles and shakes the woods. My clothes are already soaked and sticking to my body. I stand in the leaves, facing the cabin, my legs bending beneath my weight. But I will myself to keep standing; I don't dare move.

Water pours down my face. I squint, stealing a glance at the gun, trying to find the safety to make sure it's locked. My fingertip flips the switch—it wasn't. My whole body trembles.

There's a large flash against the dark sky; my vision blurs from the mix of rain and tears.

All of a sudden, the cabin door flies open, startling me.

Dad's in the doorway. I'm shaking so hard the gun rattles in my hands.

Within seconds, he's rushing toward me. I lower my face and hunch my shoulders, trying to curl into myself. Trying to protect myself.

"Rebel?" Dad says, his voice changed. There's another flash across the sky as I look up and see the question in his eyes.

He gently pulls the gun from my unsteady hands, but it's like my fingertips are glued to it. He gives the gun an extra yank, finally freeing it.

"Rebel?" he repeats.

"Y-yes, s-sir," I say, unable to keep the stutter from my voice.

He kneads his lips and drops the gun at our feet with a damp *thud*. Dad raises an arm; I flinch automatically.

But he doesn't strike; he wraps a muscled arm around me, drawing me in. I stand stiff and trembling against his chest as he squeezes me with both arms. I'm too afraid to move, too afraid to breathe, too afraid for the next time his brain decides to hit reset.

The storm thunders and flashes around us. The rain washes over us, soaks us. But he doesn't let go.

And, for the first time ever, I hear Dad cry.

EIGHTEEN

The birds chirp and rattle, signaling the first light of day. But, with the curtains drawn shut, the cabin is still gray. I don't turn on the lights.

My elbows press into the counter. My hands barely prop the weight of my chin as I lean over, staring straight ahead, staring at what I've made—the thing I thought was going to help Dad understand me better. But that all went out the window the moment he tossed me into the rain.

N8TE's battery indicator light shows he's fully charged. He's the only one. After what happened with Dad, a mix of exhaustion and sadness weighs on me.

We didn't talk. He didn't speak. Once we came inside, Dad went straight upstairs. I haven't seen or heard from him since. He didn't even pace.

In the meantime, I've managed to change into dry soldier clothes and stare at N8TE. That's about it.

I couldn't sleep.

Nothing like that had ever happened before. Sure, he's been angry. And maybe he's accidentally pushed me once or twice before Aunt Birdie made him stop. But what if he hadn't stopped last night? What if he hadn't snapped out of it?

I shake my head. I'm not going to let myself think about that. He did stop. And I'm fine.

The sudden clomping of his boots makes the hairs on my arms stand on end. I jump, edging away from N8TE. Which version of Dad is coming down the stairs?

When he reaches the ground floor, he pauses for a second. Dressed like me—or really, I'm dressed like him—he's wearing sunglasses, even though it's not bright inside. He carries the gun he forced on me last night. My blood thrums as he moves closer, my tense reflection growing larger in his mirrored lenses.

He brushes past me and into the kitchen and then spins my direction. I gasp. I can't see his eyes or, worse, predict his mood.

Without warning, he drops the magazine full of bullets

from his weapon into the palm of his hand and places it on the empty countertop. He then pulls the charging handle, showing me the inside so I can see the chamber is empty.

I try to breathe. His gun isn't loaded. Dad places his weapon on the counter next to the sink, across from N8TE, and pulls the trigger with a quiet *click*. I force myself to take another breath, attempting to slow my racing heart.

As it is, the gun can't fire now. But he doesn't stop there: He pulls the pins and separates the upper and lower parts of the gun. The lower part is soon on the countertop. The upper remains in his hand as he removes the bolt carrier group and charging handle and then places all of the pieces next to one another. He's pretty much disassembled his weapon.

Both of his hands grab the edge of the counter while his chin drops to his chest with a heavy sigh. "I don't know what happened," he says, his voice low, "but it won't happen again." He looks from the floor to me, and I can see my stunned reflection in his sunglasses.

I quickly shift my expression to neutral and nod.

He gestures to N8TE. "You've been busy."

I want to tell him I made this new robot to show him who I really am and what I really want to be doing. Instead, I point to the table and say, "So have you."

Dad pulls off his shades and glances over at his war scene. "I can't get it out of my head," he says as he walks to the table and stares.

Slowly, I move to the opposite end of the table. "Someone once told me talking about things makes them easier."

He closes his eyes and flinches, as if reliving the scene in real time.

I ease toward him and point to the toy soldier, the one standing in the front seat of the Jeep. "Is that you?"

Dad's eyes fly open; his gaze darts to the one pointing the gun at the girl. He sniffs loudly and then nods.

"Who is she?"

He shrugs and pulls out a chair; the legs scrape against the raw wood floor. "Just a girl," he says and then sits. "I don't know her name. She was about your age."

My hands clench as I debate whether to ask or not. But I can't help it: I have to know. "Did you kill her?"

He gives a brief nod.

"Why?" I ask, trying to keep my voice steady.

"She was there," Dad says, shaking his head. "We'd come out of the city." He points to the smoking rubble in the scene. "We were exhausted from two days of fighting. The enemy had civilian bombers—mostly women and children." He stops to rub his eyes, his fingers moving in circles. "I thought she had a bomb in the sack," Dad explains, his fingers slowly falling from his face. His eyes are red. "I made a split-second decision, and I shot her before she could kill me and my men."

"But she wasn't a bomber," I say, guessing.

"No. Groceries fell from her sack when she—" He takes a sharp breath, stopping himself. "I didn't have a choice," he says, his voice flat.

I nod, because what else can I do? I don't agree with what Dad did. How could I? I also don't disagree. He thought he was protecting himself and his friends.

Dad dabs the corner of one eye with his knuckle, and it seems like he's not so sure, either. Maybe that's why he keeps rebuilding this scene. He made a split-second decision, and now he has to live with it.

Josiah was right: War really does mess with a person's head.

Dad clears his throat and taps the edge of the table; grains of sand fall onto the floor. "What do you say we go outside?"

"Now?" I asked, surprised.

"I could use the fresh air." Dad stands and pushes the chair under the table. "If I remember correctly, I owe you a fishing trip." He tries a smile, looking a little more like the young man in the pictures before he went off to war.

But what if he goes off again? I knead my lips, unsure.

"Look, I know things went too far last night, and I'm really sorry. I promise I'll do better." Dad slides his hands inside his pockets. "What do you say?" he asks, his voice ebbing as if his confidence is barely hanging on.

He's waiting for me to decide: I can accept his invitation or turn away. But, there's not really a choice. Not when you love someone.

I smile. "I think that's a great idea."

***

We've been hiking and exploring and fishing all day. It's twilight, and the frogs bellow their songs along the creek. Dad crouches by the water, gutting and cleaning the trout he's caught with a makeshift fishing rod made of a long twig, plus the line, bobber, and hook from his bug-out bag.

I'm sitting on the warm ground, leaning against my backpack. I stare at Calliope's fallen log, thinking of her and her meadow of flowers on the other side of the water and through the trees. I haven't seen her since she told me I needed to speak to my dad. I shift on my elbows. I wish I could talk to her now.

"Almost ready," Dad says, a smile to his voice.

Dad and I already dug a shallow pit on this side of the creek. About the size of a round platter, we've encircled it with rocks we retrieved from the bottom of the stream. I take the large hunting knife from my bag and carve bark from a twig. Once it's clear of bark, I keep pushing my blade along the grain, down with the point of the knife, again and again, feathering the wood.

Dad approaches, holding two large and perfect filets, one resting in each hand. "Get me the skillet, will you?"

I put my knife point-side into the earth and roll to my knees, opening the top flap of Dad's bug-out bag. I dig under his gas mask, dehydrated food, and the plastic survival blanket until I reach the small cast-iron skillet at the bottom. "Here," I say, offering it to him.

Dad carefully lays the filets skin-side against the pan. "I put an onion in the outer pocket," he says, gesturing.

I set the skillet on the ground and, as he rinses his hands in the creek, I find the white onion and a pack of dehydrated strawberries. My stomach grumbles. "Can I have one?" I ask.

As he returns, Dad shakes the water from his fingers and takes the onion from me with a nod.

He sits, and I open the packet before popping a dried strawberry into my mouth. Instantly, the sweetness melts into my tongue. I'm tempted to take another one, but Dad's usually protective of his food stash. I force myself to savor the one and return the packet to his bag.

Seated next to me, Dad places the onion on the flat side of one of the logs stacked next to the pit. He chops the onion, releasing the strong smell.

I place the feathered twigs I've made into the pit with the other wood, making a nest for the fire.

"Where did you learn to do that?" he asks, stopping for a second, admiring the fringed pieces.

I swallow the last bits of the strawberry. "Mom," I say. "The feathering helps the fire get more oxygen."

Dad smiles. "I know. Do you want to start the fire?"

I'll probably bumble it if he's watching. I shake my head. "That's okay."

He passes me the onion to finish.

As I chop, I smile to myself. "Remember when Mom made the tray of caramel apples for Halloween, but she—"

"Made one of them a caramel onion?" he finishes with a laugh. "I don't know how she did it, but it looked like an apple." He unsnaps the pocket on his vest, and from the chest pocket, removes a small baggie filled with cotton balls soaked in petroleum jelly.

I grin at the memory. "And then Aunt Birdie took that huge bite."

Dad laughs. "I've never seen someone spit something so far, so fast across a room before or since."

"Me either," I say.

He takes one of the cotton balls from the baggie and pulls at it, exposing the dry fibers in the middle. He sets it between my feathered twigs.

"I think she brushed her teeth about fifty times after that."

"Oh, at least," Dad says, striking a piece of flint against the steel on his knife, making it spark. Once, twice, and the cotton ball ignites. He blows on the small fire until it spreads to my feathered pieces and then adds some dry leaves as tinder to the pit. The fire crackles and smokes a little.

I scoot over to help as he unrolls a small section of chicken wire and places it over the pit like the surface of a grill. When we're finished, he holds out the bag of strawberries. "Want some more?"

With a nod, I center the skillet of trout and onions onto the chicken wire over the fire.

He shakes dried strawberry bits into his hand and then into my cupped hands. "Thanks," I say, and we both lean against our packs, watching the fire.

I pop another sweet bite into my mouth, letting my spit dissolve it on my tongue.

He chews for a second and then stops. "Did I ever tell you what your mom did to the orange juice?"

"No," I say, sitting up, excited he actually wants to talk about Mom for a change.

"You were a baby, and we were hardly getting any sleep." He smiles. "You couldn't get your days and nights straight."

I nod.

"Anyway, I'd fed you a bottle and was carrying you downstairs so your mom could get some rest." Dad pulls one leg to his chest and wraps a hand around his knee. "I grabbed the pitcher of orange juice from the refrigerator and poured a big glass." He shakes his head with a smile. "I took a drink, thinking, *This sure tastes funny*, but I was so tired, I took another drink to make sure. Then I heard the laughter coming from the bottom of the stairs."

"Who was laughing?"

"Who do you think?" Dad winks at me.

"Mom?"

"You got it. You know that powdered cheese stuff in the macaroni and cheese boxes?" He mimics pouring and stirring.

I cover my mouth in delighted disgust.

"Yep," Dad says with a nod. "She mixed the stuff in water and put it in the orange juice pitcher." He shakes his head.

"Seriously?" I ask.

He nods. "Here we were, bone tired, but your mom never lost her sense of humor."

The tasty smell of fish and onions waft from the skillet as I look across the river. "I miss her."

"I know," Dad says, his voice softening. "I miss her, too."

I snatch a large piece of rough bark I'd carved from one of the twigs and toss it like a Frisbee. It lands on the edge of the creek with a *plunk*. "She liked to show you her funny side, since that's what she thought you needed."

Dad shifts.

"She worried about you. Constantly." I watch the flames beneath the skillet. "I worry, too."

He scoots around the fire and lays a hand on my shoulder. "You shouldn't worry. I'm making a lot of progress."

I shrug off his hand.

Dad sighs. "I know I messed up, but look at us now: fishing and cooking out." He looks skyward to where the first stars are peeking between the branches. "We're out in nature, and I haven't felt this good in a really long time." He points. "And I couldn't do this without you."

I shake my head, doubtful.

"You deserve to know you're helping me." He seems so genuine.

"I just want you to be happy again."

"I *am* happy. Can't you see?"

I'm not sure I can see it. But what I can see is the fallen log, which leads to her.

Calliope says I need to talk to him, and I know she's right. But, sitting here, with Dad so close, his eyes begging me to see how happy he is, I can't. Not right now.

"I can see it," I fib.

Dad's smile is instant. "Everything will be alright. You'll see," he says. "You have to trust me."

I take a deep breath and nod, hoping he's right.

NINETEEN

I sit on the center of the fallen log, my hands pressing into the rough and peeling bark. Yesterday with Dad—fishing and hiking—was perfect. The whole day, it was only the two of us. No Wade. No Karl. No Dwight. No guns. No drills. Just us. And Dad really did seem happy.

I know I told Calliope I'd talk to him, but I couldn't. It had been so long since he'd actually seemed to enjoy being with me; I didn't have the heart to ruin it.

He promised me things would get better, and I really want to believe him. It already is better.

My heavy boots swing side to side a couple of feet above the bubbling creek. From the treetops on either side of the stream, the birds call to one another. I breathe deep as the breeze shifts, and I get a whiff of lemons and honey. "Hey, Calliope."

She appears, wide-eyed, from between the trees on the left bank. "How'd you know it was me?" With her fishing pole in one hand, she's wearing a flowery shirt and jean shorts. There's a canvas bag covered with patches slung across her body.

"Lucky guess," I say, glad she's actually talking to me, instead of running the opposite direction.

Calliope reaches the edge of the water. "Did you know honeybees sense when a storm is coming?"

"Hmmm," I say, smiling at her new piece of trivia. "So since I knew it was you, I guess that makes me the bee." Then I point to her with a smile. "And you're the storm?"

"I think it's the other way around." She shakes her head. "No, the bees hide in the hive so they don't get wet." A sly grin brightens her face; she points to her backside. "As I recall, you don't mind getting wet." She laughs, clearly making fun of me for falling in the damp grass during our soccer match.

I put my hands up. "Okay, okay, I knew I didn't have a chance of winning. But it was the only way I could keep you from leaving."

"You didn't keep me. I chose to stay and kick your butt."

"*Hey,*" I say.

She pulls a small baggie from the front pocket of her bag. "Sheep are the same way, you know?"

"What? They stink at soccer?"

"No, they gather before a storm so they can shield each other from the rain. There's a saying: 'When sheep gather in a huddle, tomorrow we'll have a puddle.'"

I grin. "Do you really get all this stuff from watching *Jeopardy!*?"

She shrugs and opens the baggie, removing something flat and slimy and pink.

I turn up my nose. "What's that?"

"Raw bacon," she says, tearing off a small piece before placing it on her hook. "The fish love it."

"Gross."

Calliope returns the sealed baggie to her bag. "You don't like bacon?"

"Who doesn't like bacon?"

She nods with approval. "I guess you're not as weird as you look."

I laugh and then shift. Does she really think I'm weird-looking? "I don't think people are allowed to say those kinds of things."

"What?"

"That someone looks weird." I tug on the collar of my black T-shirt. "It's a little rude."

"Why? I'm weird-looking."

I stop tugging on my shirt and shake my head. "You're definitely not. You're—" I glance at her eyelashes, her large brown eyes, her long legs, and the curls framing her confident jaw.

She clears her throat. "Yes?"

I wipe my hands on my pants.

Calliope tilts her head and stares straight at me. Maybe straight through me. I only hope she's not doing the Jedi mind thing again and reading my mind.

"I guess you aren't *that* weird-looking," she says.

"Thanks a lot."

"Any time," she says and then plunks her bacon hook into the stream. She stares into the clear water, watching her bait swish back and forth. "Though I'm not really a fan of the new clothes."

"What?" I ask, joking. I pull the sides of my camo pants. "You don't like me looking like an avatar from *Call of Duty*?"

Calliope focuses on the red bobber in the water, her voice softer. "You still look like one of them."

My smile falls. "I'm *not* one of them."

"You never answered my question the other day."

I don't know what she's talking about.

She looks up at me. "Why are you even here then if you're not one of them?"

Her question stings. I put the sole of my shoe on the log. "I can leave if you want."

"Yes, you're quite good at that." She shakes her head. "No, I'm just trying to understand: You *say* you don't believe what they do, but you're staying at their camp, and you dress like them, and I want to know why."

"I already told you," I say, defensive. "I'm here because of my dad."

"Who's one of them, right?"

My shoulders tense.

"I don't know," she says. "I don't get it: If you don't like it here, why don't you stay home with your mom?"

It's like she's knocked me on my butt again.

She points to the top of the waterfall. "Unless she's up there being a racist with the rest of them?"

My jaw tightens. "I guess Josiah didn't tell you: She's dead."

Calliope's expression immediately shifts.

My fingernails dig into the bark. "And she wasn't a racist," I say, loud. "She was the kindest person I've ever known."

"He didn't tell me," she says. "I didn't know." She bores the toe of her shoe into the ground. "I thought you said your mom gave you that *Minecraft* shirt."

"She did," I say, curt. "Which is why I still wear it, even though I know I'm way too old for it."

She cringes. "I didn't think to ask." She pushes the end of the fishing pole into the mud. "I'm sorry."

I nod, my breath slowing. "I guess I have the opposite problem. I think too much and never speak when I should." I watch the bacon hook skate under the surface as she hops onto the log.

The bark makes a scratching sound as she scoots near the center and sits a few inches from me. Her red tennis shoes dangle next to my shiny boots. "Can I ask what happened to her?" Her voice is gentle against the roll of the creek.

"Heart attack." I glance at the patches of blue sky, peeking between the branches. "She wasn't even forty yet, but I think all those years of stress got to her." I shift my weight on the log. "My dad was always in danger; plus, he was a different person every time he came home from one of his tours of duty." I nod to myself. "She still loved him, though. She was always trying to take care of him."

"Like you," Calliope notes.

I shrug. "I guess."

"I'm sorry about your mom. Really."

I let out a sad laugh. "I guess it's sort of ironic."

"What?" she asks.

"My dad was the one who was always in danger, but he's the one who survived."

Calliope nods, and we sit for several seconds, maybe several minutes, letting the creek wash away my words when I finally face her.

She's looking at the water, her hair a thick curtain across her cheek.

"Can I ask you something?"

She nods.

"What happened to your parents?"

"I don't know," she says.

My insides twist with disappointment. "It's okay, you don't have to tell me."

"No, I really don't know what happened to them. I was literally dropped on the doorstep of Josiah's church when I was a baby."

"Really?"

"Really," she says with a firm nod. "Josiah was practicing his sermon in the pulpit when he heard me crying." She smiles a little. "He says I sounded like a tiny lamb and was no bigger than a peanut."

I grin. "Is that why he calls you 'Peanut'?"

"You guessed it."

"And why you call him by his name, instead of 'Grandpa'?"

"Right again." She tucks a strand of hair behind her ear. "I never knew Josiah's wife, though. She had already died when I came into the picture. But Josiah says I was his little miracle. He says God saw how lonely he was and sent me to help."

"I can see that."

She lifts her long legs straight over the water and stares at her knees. "I still look for them, though—my parents." She lowers her legs. "When I was little, I used to stop people all the time and ask."

"You did?"

"As you can probably guess, it was a little awkward for Josiah. People would give us both a strange look." She shifts. "But sometimes when he prays during Sunday service, I'll still look around the congregation to see if I look like one of them. Or I'll check the faces at the farmers market." She tugs a thread on the bottom of her shorts. "It's stupid, I know, but I can't help it. It's been over thirteen years; I doubt they're coming back for me now."

"You never know," I say, gently nudging her shoe with mine.

"Maybe you haven't heard: Grown-ups don't really like teenagers."

"I like you," I say.

"But you're not a grown-up," she notes.

"True, but I like you," I say again. "And that has to count for something."

She gives me a strange look, raised eyebrow and all.

And suddenly, I realize how it sounds. I like her. My neck goes hot. I drop my legs against the log. "I mean—as a friend—I like—"

"I know what you mean," she says, saving me.

This is why I don't say what I'm thinking.

"So." She scratches her knee. "I brought you something."

"You're kidding." I carefully move my leg, straddling the log like a horse, so I can face her.

"I guess Josiah's giving me a conscience or something." She smiles. "I felt bad after I kicked your butt at soccer."

I laugh. "Rub it in, why don't you?"

She leans over to pull something from her canvas bag. "Here," she says and hands me a comic book.

"No way." It's the same Han Solo comic I was admiring at the farmers market. "How did you find this?"

"I asked Old Mick if he still had it," she says. "He said it's from 1997, so totally vintage."

"Wow." My fingers run across the dark space scene on the cover. "I don't know what to say."

"Thank you usually works pretty well."

"Thank you," I say. "Wow, thank you so much."

She nods with a smile. "You're welcome."

I flip through the pages, admiring the old advertisements for Dragon Con and collectible sculptures from *The X-Files*.

Calliope nudges the book. "Can I ask *you* something?"

I nod, closing the comic. "Of course."

"Did you talk to your dad?"

Her question hovers in the air between us. I don't want to ruin this. I'd rather talk about the comic book. Or bees. Or sheep. Anything. But she expects an answer and, of all people, she deserves one. "I tried," I finally answer and brace for the disappointment I already see forming on her face. "Calliope—"

"It's fine," she says, cutting me off. "I knew you wouldn't. And you didn't."

I stiffen, offended she already knew I couldn't do it. "Then why did you bring me this?" I ask, holding the comic.

Calliope puts the sole of her shoe on the log, pushing to stand. "I gotta go."

Heat flickers. "I thought *I* was the one who was always running away."

She's already moving across the log.

I bumble to stand, but my foot gets caught as I'm swinging it over the log. I'm falling sideways; my arm flails and connects with Calliope's ankle.

She gasps.

We both lose our balance. My hand shoots up in the air, trying to keep my comic book dry before the splash.

Cold water bubbles inside my ears. I hurriedly sit up and suck in a breath. My comic book is still dry.

Calliope stands over me, also dry, except for the bottom of her legs. Of course she landed on her feet.

The water flows around my waist. "Well, *this* is humiliating," I say and shake my wet head.

She snorts a laugh and then tries to hold it in.

"Are you laughing at me?" I say, which only makes her laugh harder. And even though I'm cold and soaking, her laughter makes me feel warm inside.

"Here," she says, taking the comic from me and offering her other hand. "Let me help you."

I take it and stand, water rushing away from my body. She releases me, and I try to wring out the bottom of my T-shirt, but it's no use. The water nudges my calves; I wedge my boot against a rock, trying to keep my balance.

"Steady," she says, keeping her hands out, as if she's ready to grab me in case I fall again.

Why is she always helping me? Why is she still smiling at me when I'm so clumsy and stupid? I know I don't deserve it, and she should know why. "You asked me why I'm here."

The smile leaves her face; she wipes a water droplet from her cheek and nods.

"I did something," I say, curling my hands into fists. "It's bad, and you're probably going to hate me and never want to talk to me again."

She rolls the comic in her hands, unblinking, expecting my confession. I wish she'd tell me it doesn't matter. But clearly it does.

"I got expelled," I blurt before I can change my mind, and it sounds so final when I say it. "My best friend, Ajeet—I spray-painted a message on his locker." My hands are balled so tight, I can feel my fingernails cutting into my hands. "I was upset, but I shouldn't have done it." I shudder, thinking of the red letters.

"What did you write?"

"It's awful."

"Tell me."

I sigh. "Go back to your own country."

Calliope bites her bottom lip.

"But I didn't mean it," I argue, opening my hands. "I was so upset. Dad didn't get the job he wanted, and he wouldn't listen to me about what I wanted."

"So you decided to write hate speech on your best friend's locker?" she says, her voice full of judgment.

I lower my head in shame, watching the clear water flow between my ankles. "I don't know what I was thinking. I don't want to be like him, okay?" I look into her dark eyes. "I don't want to be filled with hate like he is or spread hate or any of that stuff. I don't want to be so angry all the time."

"Then, don't be," Calliope says matter-of-factly.

I scoff. "It's not that easy."

"Nothing important ever is." She crosses her arms over her chest. "And you probably aren't going to like hearing this."

I dig my feet into the silt, trying to ready myself for the blow. "What?"

"You already *are* spreading hate."

I stagger a little.

"You have a habit of not speaking up when you should," she says. "It's like Josiah said: Complacency is just as bad." She lifts a finger. "If you remain silent, you're telling the hater you're okay with what he's saying and doing."

"But I'm not okay with it," I say, defensive. "Any of it."

Her arms fall to her sides. "Then why don't you say some-thing?"

I think of Dad and his temper. I shiver. "It's not that easy," I say again.

She lets out a dry laugh. "*Easy?* You're not seriously going to talk to me about what's easy, are you? Have you ever been given the stink-eye or followed around when you walk into a store because of the color of your skin? Have you ever feared for your life when you see a police officer because you can't know what judgments he's already made because of the way you look?"

"I didn't mean it like that." I shake my head. "All I'm trying to say is it's hard when the hater is someone you love. Someone you're supposed to respect."

"But are you really loving him if you're lying to him?"

I flinch. I hadn't thought of it that way before.

"You're not helping anyone by staying quiet, especially not yourself." She moves from the water onto the bank and jos-tles the fishing line. The bacon hook sways toward a passing fish, but he doesn't bite. "Josiah says God calls each of us to respond to what we're meant to be, and if we don't, we can never truly be happy." She wipes a hand across her mouth and then sighs. "Rebel, maybe it's time for you to respond."

"And what if I don't go to church? What then? Do you really think God cares about me?"

She nods. "God still wants you to be who you were meant to be. Don't you?"

"Sure, but I also want my dad to like me for me, and not what he thinks I should be." I push air between my lips, frustrated all over again. "That sounds so stupid, doesn't it?"

"No," Calliope answers. "But sometimes you can still love someone even though you don't like them very much."

"What if I want him to love me *and* like me?"

Her face softens as she moves into the current. My heart runs as she wades knee-deep into the creek. She hands me the comic. "If you're true to yourself, you'll be okay." To my surprise, she takes my other hand and squeezes.

Sunlight filters across her face. My chest fills with warmth. Her dark eyes sparkle and then change in an instant, like she's seen a ghost.

She yanks her hand away and turns, water sloshing as she hurries onto the bank.

It's worse than a Band-Aid being ripped from my skin. "I'm sorry," I say, clumsily splashing toward her, wondering what I did wrong this time.

"You led them here," she says.

"Who?" I call after her, my shins pushing against the moving water until I reach the bank. "Please don't go," I beg. But she's already disappearing between the trees when, out of nowhere, I hear something drop in the leaves. Goose bumps race along my skin. Slowly, I turn in my soggy boots.

Karl stands at the top of the rock wall. There's a pair of fishing poles at his feet.

Dad lands with a *thud* at the bottom of the waterfall, his anger zeroing in on me. I freeze on the muddy bank as he glowers, every muscle tight. Ready to attack.

TWENTY

I'm clutching the Star Wars comic book tightly in my hand. Dad is already halfway across the creek, slogging toward the bank where I stand frozen. Water soaks the bottoms of his pant legs, yet he keeps perfect balance.

Karl descends the rocks next to the waterfall and lands on the other bank. My instincts tell me to turn and run. But if I do, I'll lead them straight to Calliope, and I can't do that. I won't do that.

Dad's boots squish onto the shore; he's bulging—his muscles, his veins. He rips Calliope's fishing pole from the ground and snaps it in two over his thigh. I wince as he tosses part of it aside; the bacon hook and half of the pole float downstream in the current. Dad grips the other half of the wooden pole, the broken end sharp like a spear. "I told you to stay away from her," he barks. "What did you tell her?"

I edge backward.

"You're feeding her information, aren't you?" His eyes dart.

I quickly shake my head.

"When are they coming for us?"

"Who?" I ask, totally confused.

He scoffs. "Oh, you really are good. You know who I'm talking about."

From the corner of my eye, I spot Karl shuffling across the log. All of a sudden, I realize who. "The New World Order?"

"Ha! I knew it!"

"Dad, please. I'm not talking to them." I put a hand against my chest. "It's just me: Rebel."

"You're a traitor," Dad says, raising the pole over his head, ready to strike.

I close my eyes, bracing for the blow, forcing myself to stay still. *I can't run. I can't lead them to Calliope and Josiah.*

I hear the high-pitched whip of the pole through the air, followed by a smack. There's a grunt and scuffle.

"Nathan, stop!"

My eyes fly open as Karl grips Dad's wrist. There's a red whip mark along Karl's pale arm. He shakes the pole to the ground, disarming my dad.

Dad reaches, but he's not fast enough.

Karl snatches the remaining piece of Calliope's fishing pole and flings it into the creek with a *plunk*. "Enough!" Karl yells.

Dad digs his boot into the shore, the mud squelching before he shoves Karl in the chest. Karl staggers, but holds his ground.

My heart races.

Dad turns his narrow focus to me.

"Stand down, soldier," Karl commands.

Dad looks ready to charge.

My knees buckle; my butt's on the ground. The comic slips from my hand. My fingers dig into the cool mud as I try to scoot away.

"That's an order, Sergeant!"

There's a sudden shift in Dad's expression. He blinks as if he's been awakened. He examines his surroundings—the sky, the water, the trees.

Me.

My heart is beating so loud, I can't even hear the creek.

With one eye on Dad, Karl carefully approaches and offers me a hand.

I'm shaking, but I take it—he holds on tight—and I let him pull me from the ground. I can sense Dad staring at the comic book, full focus. I want to hide it. Protect it.

"You okay?" Karl asks, still holding me upright.

I nod, even though I'm not. It's all I can do not to collapse again.

Dad is breathing heavy; his chest heaves as he bends toward my comic book.

No, don't touch it. I don't want him to touch it. To spoil it.

He snatches it. "Did she give this to you?" he asks, his voice low and accusing.

I don't answer. I don't know how to answer.

"These things make you soft. They brainwash you into thinking the world's full of heroes."

I want to tell him he was my hero. But before I get the chance, he throws my comic book into the creek.

The pages sag from the weight of the water. The colors begin to run. The words disappear.

"You will *never* see her again, that's an order," he barks as I watch the current sweep part of me away.

***

The side of my rib cage presses against the hard futon as my brain revolves between embarrassment over what Dad did at the creek into anger and finally into fear of what he might do next. What would have happened if Karl hadn't stepped in?

When we returned to camp, Karl made Dad stay away

from me until he knew I would be safe. It took several hours.

I'm seething again.

Dad is pacing upstairs. He's been pacing all night. Each of his footfalls lands with a *thump*, followed by a shuddering creak, like the cabin is complaining about our lack of sleep.

I huff and roll onto my back, glaring at the wood ceiling. From the corner of my eye, I catch a glimpse of the muted sunlight lining the outer edges of the blackout curtains.

I can't believe he scared off Calliope and then threw my comic book into the water. So what if it makes me "soft"?

I'm tired of being on edge all the time, not knowing which Dad is in front of me. I'm tired of the whirlwind, set to rapid repeat in an unpredictable cycle of anger, fear, sadness, love, anger, fear, sadness, love. . . .

I want to talk to him. Tell him how I feel. But every time I try, I either don't have the heart to ruin the rare moment he seems happy *or* it's like I'm not looking at my dad at all, but a soldier who's decided I'm another enemy in need of destruction.

Thump, creak. Thump, creak.

My hands cover my face in frustration as I think about what Calliope said: *If you remain silent, you're telling the hater you're okay with what he's saying and doing.*

I exhale. But I'm not okay with what he's doing. We came here so he'd get better. So he could see the real me. But I've never felt more hidden.

And now I'm worried I'm in way over my head here. I have to do something.

I throw off the thin blanket before I can change my mind. "Dad," I call, sitting up. I push the balls of my bare feet into the wood floor.

Within seconds, footsteps thump across the ceiling and move toward the stairs. "What's wrong?" Dad asks, looking stressed as he reaches the bottom floor. He's fully dressed and carrying our bug-out bags.

"Nothing," I say and take a deep breath, trying to stay calm, hoping he'll take a hint and do the same.

He drops the packs at the base of the stairs and flips the light on over my futon.

I squint and spot his uneasiness from a few feet away. I'm sweating already; the backs of my knees stick to the sheet.

"Are you hurt?" Dad asks as he nears.

I rub my damp palms onto my shorts. "I—I need to talk to you."

Dad's body remains tight, defensive, as he approaches the table with his war scene and pulls out a chair. He turns the chair and sits, facing me with his arms crossed over his chest. "Talk."

I take another breath, shifting on the mattress. "I think we should leave."

"Leave," Dad repeats, his voice monotone.

"This place is not what I thought it was going to be. I thought we were going to—I don't know—do stuff together."

Irritation flashes across his face. "Didn't I take the entire day off to go hiking and fishing?"

"You did," I say with an abrupt nod. "But you're always doing stuff for them."

"Them?" he asks. Dad crosses his ankles to match his arms, closing off completely. "Those men are our comrades."

"Maybe they're yours," I say. "But they're not helping you."

Dad pokes his tongue against the inside of his mouth, pushing out his cheek, like he's trying to control his temper.

I snag my pillow from the head of the bed and squish it onto my lap.

"So you'd have me go back to being jobless, unable to support my family?"

"We were doing fine with Aunt Birdie."

"It's not her job to support us," he says, his voice rising.

"But I miss her, and I want to be able to go to school." My

fingers curl around the edges of the pillow. "I miss the real world."

Dad sucks in his cheeks for a second and points to the floor. "This *is* the real world. We're preparing for a takeover the rest of the world is too blind to see."

I roll my eyes.

"You're so naive," he chides.

I hold my pillow like a shield. "I'm not naive," I say and then toss it aside. "I just don't see how any of this is helping you get better. You still don't sleep. You're angry all the time." I stop myself from saying: *I'm afraid for you. I'm afraid of you.* I sigh. "You don't get it: I'm never going to be like you."

"So you'd rather give up than survive?"

My muscles tense; heat courses through my veins as I jump from the futon. "Everything isn't about surviving."

In an instant, he pops up, knocking over the chair. My feet slide backward across the floor; the backs of my knees hit the edge of the futon. Dad stomps into the kitchen, snatching N8TE from the counter. The cord dangles from its charging port.

"What are you doing?" I ask.

Dad looks at N8TE with disgust. "The first thing the New World Order is going to do is cut the power grid. Do you think this *thing* will help you when that happens?" He yanks the trash can from under the sink.

"What are you doing?" I ask, a little louder.

He chucks N8TE, and it feels like I've been punched in the chest. First my comic book, now this? I press my lips together as he tips the crate, and all of my spare parts fall. They rattle and clunk until everything has been dumped in the trash.

Dad tosses the empty crate into the sink with a *clang*. "You don't listen. You're too wrapped up in your own make-believe world of comics and robots to see what's really happening." He rubs his temples, as if working to calm himself, but I can still see the veins popping along the sides of his neck. "If you'd pay attention for a few seconds, you'll see I'm trying to show you how to survive."

Angry heat rushes from the top of my head to the tips of my toes; it feels like I'm about to boil over. "Like you?" I ask, my hand cutting the air. "You call this surviving?"

Shock tightens his face.

"I want to do more than survive: I want to live. And so should you."

Dad shakes his head. "I thought you were happy here."

"I only pretended I was."

He flinches; something like hurt creases his face.

I take a breath and lower my voice. "Most of the time I was pretending," I say, backpedaling. "Not always."

But it's too late. "Why would you pretend?" he asks.

"Because you like it here," I say, trying to keep my voice even. Trying to keep the anger from taking over.

Dad looks me straight in the eye, and for the first time, it's like he actually sees me, instead of the me he wants me to be.

And I don't think he likes it. His face twists—Angry Dad.

I put out my hands in surrender. "Dad, I'm only trying to help."

The front door bursts open, startling us both.

"Attention," Karl commands.

Dad straightens automatically, his eyes fixed on a point in space over my shoulder.

I clench my hands, relieved and annoyed they're here.

Wade marches into the cabin. "At ease," he says, and Dad relaxes only a bit. Wade looks between us, as if assessing the situation. "I've come to inform you both the time has come."

I shift uncomfortably.

Wade grips the gun slung across his chest. "I've made the decision to activate Operation Mutual Defense."

My gaze flicks between Wade's stern expression and Karl's blank one and Dad's hopeful one. "What's that?" I ask.

Wade's knuckles go white around his weapon.

"It's our next mission. There's been a call to arms," Karl explains. "We'll be meeting in a few days with other militia groups around the country."

Wade turns to Dad. "Everyone needs to be packed—only the essentials—and be ready to leave by nightfall."

Nightfall? "Where are we going?"

"We need you on the front line," Wade says, "building more weapons."

I open my mouth to ask, *Weapons for what?*, but Dad shoots me a death glare.

Wade lowers his voice, speaking only to Dad. "I'd like to discuss something with you in private, soldier." His thin eyebrows lift and fall. "I have figured out a way to deal with the problem we discussed earlier."

What's he talking about? "What problem?" Dread curdles my stomach.

Wade gives a curt nod. "The war has finally begun."

TWENTY-ONE

War? What war?

Wade is the first to leave our cabin, followed by Karl. Dad trails them, stopping in the doorway for a second and glances over his shoulder. "Looks like you got your wish."

As usual, I have no idea what he's talking about.

"We're leaving," he says and then exits, closing the door behind him.

"I didn't wish for this," I say to the closed door, which is pretty much the same as talking to Dad. Neither is listening.

Another flame of frustration spreads throughout my body. I stomp toward the blue-and-white-checkered cloth and yank it across the rope. I flip on the overhead light bulb. It flickers and buzzes.

The bathroom faucet squeaks as I turn it, releasing water—brown and smelly at first—into the sink. When it clears, I splash cold water across my face and, with both hands clutching the sides of the sink, stare into the hazy mirror. What now? Water drips from my chin as I try to think what to do next. We need to go home, not on a stupid mission.

I need to make Dad listen. Tell him how crazy this all is. I don't know how, but he needs to hear me out.

I quickly brush my teeth and get ready. After pulling on my clean soldier outfit, I open the door to fresh air when I spy Karl, sitting on our porch. Without even looking at me, he pats the place on the step next to him. The butt of his AR-15 is visible, barely extending past his hip.

My heart skips a beat. For a second, I consider retreating and locking myself inside the cabin. But what good would it do when he could shoot open the lock?

I carefully sit next to Karl.

He takes the gun from his lap and hands it over. "You do good work," he says.

I slowly take his weapon, willing my hands not to tremble. I drop the magazine from the gun, disarming it. Then I set the magazine on the porch and check the chamber to make sure it's empty. It is.

"For someone who hates guns," Karl adds.

The gun snaps shut. "Who says I hate guns?"

Karl's head tilts with a long laugh, putting me even more on edge. "Please," he finally says. "When I hand a weapon to most guys, they're looking for the nearest target. They can't wait to shoot." He shakes his head. "Not you."

I nervously hand him the empty gun. "So?"

"*So*, you're a thinker. I like that about you." A wide smile spreads across his face. Karl is scary enough when he's not smiling, but he's absolutely terrifying when he grins. He looks like he's about to pull another weapon and kill me.

"I need to go." I quickly stand and hop to the ground; dry leaves *swish* at my feet. I only hope I can outrun him before he draws, but I seriously doubt it.

"What has your dad told you about Operation Mutual Defense?"

My dad? I stop and carefully face him. The gun is still in his lap. The bullets remain on the porch. I shrug. "Nothing, why?"

"How about this information Wade has for your dad? Do you know anything about that?"

It feels like he's toying with me. Shouldn't he know the answers to his questions? He is the head of security. "The first I heard of it was just now," I say, suddenly jittery. "Why? What's going on?"

He purses his lips, looking toward the woods.

I shake my head. He's exactly like Dad, ignoring my questions. *"Hello?"*

Karl shifts his weight on the step. "Are you sure you don't know why Wade's gathering all the militias outside of Washington, D.C.? Your dad hasn't mentioned anything to you?"

"Shouldn't *you* know?"

"One would think." He mindlessly slides the gun on his lap. "I was hoping since you and your dad disappeared the other day, he told you something about the mission."

Every one of my nerves is on high alert. "How'd you know we were gone?"

"It's my job to know," Karl says without blinking.

"Then isn't it also your job to know what Wade is planning?"

He laughs. "You're not as timid as you look, kid." He stands and walks through the leaves until he's only a few feet away, his voice a little softer. "Look, if he told you something, I really need to know."

"We were just hiking and fishing." I ball my hands. "Dad doesn't really talk to me much about this stuff. About anything, really."

"So I've heard," he says.

The hairs on my neck stand on end. "Wait a minute," I

say, wondering if our cabin is somehow bugged. Has he been listening to us? I shake my head, forcing my mind to stop spiraling down the paranoid trail of the Flag Bearers.

"Go ahead and ask," Karl dares. "It seems like you have pretty good instincts."

"Is our cabin bugged?" I ask and immediately wish I could take it back for how ridiculous it sounds.

Karl gives a swift nod.

No, this can't be right. "Did the Flag Bearers do it?"

"I did."

I point to him. "But, you *are* a Flag Bearer."

Karl gives the slightest shake of his head.

Wait, what? "Then who are you?"

Karl moves closer. When he's only inches away, he checks our surroundings, taking an extra second or two to look between the trees until his cool eyes land squarely on mine. "FBI."

"*FBI?*" I shriek. "Yeah, right, and I'm Jabba the Hutt."

"I need you to keep your voice down."

"Yeah, I bet," I say with a short laugh.

"I'm serious."

"Oh, you're really good."

He puts a hand out, shushing me as he cranes his neck to

listen. But all I hear is the quiet flow of the creek and the wind moving through the trees. Karl's hand drops to his side before whispering, "I'm an undercover agent, assigned to investigate the Flag Bearers."

I wipe my hands across my pants. "I don't believe you."

"Think about it," Karl says, pointing the direction of the training grounds. "These guys hate the federal government. They'd kill me in a heartbeat if they knew who I was. Do you really think I'd tell you I was an FBI agent if I wasn't?"

He has a point. Suddenly, I'm off-kilter. Dad was right all along: There really are FBI agents in the woods. "I—I don't think we should be talking."

"I need your help."

Leaves crunch behind me.

Fear seizes Karl's eyes as his gaze shifts. He draws a large knife from the sheath on his leg. I gasp as he puts a hand on my arm, shoving me behind him. He points his blade the direction of the approaching sound.

Dad rounds the cabin, stiffening when he sees us.

Karl turns toward me without skipping a beat. "And that's how you protect your comrade when you only have a knife," he announces before sheathing his blade. His eyes beg me to play along. "Got it?"

"I—I think so?"

Karl slaps me on the shoulder, a little too hard. I stumble forward. "Teaching Rebel some defensive maneuvers."

Dad nears the porch steps and stops, noticing the disassembled weapon. "Wade asked me to get the iodine tablets," he says as he bends over to grab the gun parts. "He knows I keep a few boxes on hand." Dad clicks the magazine onto the lower portion of the gun.

Karl's hand moves to his sheath.

"For water purification?" I ask, my voice wavering.

"Right," Dad says.

Karl clears his throat. "If it's alright with you, Nathan, I'd like to show your boy a few things on the training grounds before we leave." He hasn't taken his hand off the hilt of his knife.

"He's not much of a shot."

Karl grabs my shoulder; I jump. "If he's going to tag along, he needs to learn how to do more than weapons assembly. Let me teach him a few things."

Dad shrugs. "I'll need him back in about an hour to help clean and pack."

"Shouldn't be a problem," Karl says and nudges me away from the cabin, his fingers still touching the knife.

We walk a few steps before Dad calls, "Hold up."

Karl squeezes my shoulder, making me yelp.

Dad carries the reassembled gun to Karl. "You forgot."

"Wouldn't have been long before I missed it," Karl says with a false laugh as he takes the gun.

Dad glances at me for a split second; my heart races. He knows. He must know something's up. Karl is being way too nice to me.

"Let's go," Karl says, shoving me downhill, away from Dad before he can ask.

When we reach the river, Karl checks over his shoulder and slings the gun across his back. "I need your help," he whispers.

"Why me?"

"Because Wade doesn't lay out a job until right before it happens, and only to those who are involved." He gestures to the dry rock in the middle, but I refuse to cross. "I'm sure Wade told your dad about the robbery only a few hours before it happened."

My eyes widen. "You know about that?"

"Of course," he says and leaps to the rock before landing on the other side. He waits for me, a smirk on his face.

He knows about the robbery, and I was there. If this guy

really is FBI, Dad is already in trouble. I probably am, too. All of a sudden, I don't feel so good. I hop to the center rock and then across. "Am I in some kind of trouble?"

Karl forges ahead. When I catch up, his eyes are scanning the trees, checking all directions, as he speaks under his breath, "You're not in trouble unless you planned the robbery."

I immediately shake my head, keeping pace. "No, sir."

He climbs over a rock smothered in lichen; I follow. "We recently received the surveillance video from the business across the street." He's moving full speed ahead. "We know you were an innocent bystander."

"We?" I ask, getting a little winded from his rapid pace.

Karl nods, whispering, "The FBI." He waves, and I can see Dwight has spotted us through the trees. He's carrying boxes, labeled DEHYDRATED FOOD, across the clearing.

"About a third of the warehouse is empty," Dwight reports to Karl as we exit the trees. "We should have it done in the next hour, sir."

"Very good," Karl says, and Dwight walks away. Karl hands me his gun. "Here, safety's off. Stay here." He turns and climbs up the watchtower ladder.

As he ascends, I flip the safety with my finger and try to breathe. Karl is an FBI agent, posing as head of security for a racist, anti-government militia. I almost laugh at the irony: They forgot to watch the most important watchman of all—their own.

Before I know it, Karl is standing in front of me again with another gun in his hand, a handgun tucked in his waistband, along with the knife on his leg. He must keep a stash of weapons in the watchtower. "Shall we?" he says, gesturing toward the training grounds.

Morgan and some of the other kids are peeling paper targets from the gun range, while Justin lifts one of the barrels inside the fence line.

"Leave it," Karl commands. "We'll scrap it later. Go help your dad gather the grenades."

Grenades?

"Yes, sir," Justin says, dropping the barrel before running to his next assignment.

I shake my head, whispering, "I bet he wouldn't be so eager to follow orders if he knew you were FBI."

Karl shoots me a stern look.

"There's something I don't get, though," I say, ignoring his glare. "If you already know about the robbery, why haven't you arrested everyone?"

He nudges me toward the fence, speaking under his breath, "First of all, we just received the video evidence." He leaps over the fence and ducks behind a barrel, expecting me to join him. It takes me a second, but when I finally make it over, he whispers, "Second, I'm getting close. I can feel it." He nods, sticking in his earplugs. "Ears."

Huh?

Oh, *earplugs*. I don't have mine.

Karl sighs in frustration and searches his pockets until he finds an extra pair inside his shirt. He pushes them into the meat of my hand. "I've been investigating these guys for about nine months now; they're funding all kinds of racist groups. And there's something about to go down, bigger than a robbery."

"What?" I ask, nervous all over again.

Karl taps his ear, and I hurriedly shove the plugs in mine, muffling the sound of his first gunshot. *Boom!* A perfect shot in the middle of the target's skull.

He moves to the next barrel and gestures for me to join him. I run and land on my knees before he turns to me, speaking under his breath, "Like I said: Wade is pretty paranoid. He'll let me know things when he thinks I need to know them, but I'm afraid it might be too late."

"So why don't you bug his cabin, too?" I ask.

"Can't," Karl answers. "Paranoid son of a gun sweeps the place three times a day. Besides, he's always moving when he's

giving assignments. Always outside. Always different places."
Karl shakes his head. "I can't bug every tree in the woods."
He stops and peeks over the barrel, checking our surroundings, before he comes back down, whispering, "Something big is about to happen once we meet up with the others, and your dad's involved in whatever that is. Innocent people are going to get hurt if we don't stop them."

"*We?*"

He points between us. "You and me."

I bristle. Dad wouldn't hurt innocent people, especially after all the regret he's had over that girl. "My dad wouldn't hurt innocent people," I argue.

"You sure?" Karl shoots again.

I jump and then check: The hole's in the heart of his target. He nods at me, as if expecting me to shoot.

With trembling hands, I raise the weapon. "Safety!" Karl shouts.

I startle, but flip the switch and quickly pull the trigger. *Bam!* The butt of the gun slams against my shoulder. The smell of gunpowder burns my nose. I'm definitely getting a bruise.

"You need to wrap your body around it more. Are you even looking through the scope?" he asks and then runs toward the kill house, where Dwight shot the child's picture.

Look through the scope?

He flings open the door to the house and ducks behind it before taking another shot. Again, in the skull of the target. He looks to me.

I try not to think about the gun in my hands and run forward again, landing near the outside door behind Karl.

He puts two fingers to his eyes and then gestures for us to move forward.

"Two targets?" I ask, and he nods before taking one shot. A second. He hits the targets perfectly.

Karl pulls out his earplugs and waits for me to do the same before speaking in a normal voice. "The key is to line your target in the crosshairs of the scope."

I glance through the scope and see the black lines forming a cross.

"Your target should be sitting on top of the notch at the front of your weapon." He pushes on the end of the gun.

I nod.

"Try it?" he asks, returning the plugs to his ears.

I press my lips together as I push the earplugs in and force myself still. Wrapping my body around the weapon, I pull the butt of the gun into my shoulder and look through the scope toward the target. Without thinking too hard, I shoot. My ears ring.

"Better," Karl says.

My heart races. I check: It's glanced off the paper target's shoulder. I'm a little light-headed.

"Wade's enacted Operation Mutual Defense," Karl says softly before rounding the corner. He squats behind a wall in the center of the kill house.

"What does that mean?" I ask, jostling the gun as I huddle close so I can hear him without removing my earplugs again.

"It's a call to arms to militia groups around the country. The plan is—in five days—everyone will be gathering near Washington, D.C."

"What's in Washington?"

"I'm supposed to meet Wade at a hotel there and await further instructions." He shrugs. "That's all I know, and I'm afraid by the time I get there, it'll be too late to get my guys in place."

I slide to my butt, sitting on the cool packed dirt. "So why are you telling me this?"

"Because your dad knows something. And I'd bet you my life Wade's talked to him about what they're going to do once we get to Washington."

"And you want me to ask my dad what's going on and report back to you?"

Karl nods.

I can't believe it: He's asking me to snitch on my dad. "So you can arrest him." I shake my head. "Forget it." I rise to my feet.

Karl grabs my arm, stopping me. "It will save lives, Rebel."

I shake free. "My dad wouldn't hurt innocent people," I say a little louder than I mean to.

Karl puts a finger over his lips and checks around the corners of the kill house.

"I know he likes his guns," I say, a little softer. "And he can be a big talker, but he's a hero—a real one. He's a hero," I repeat.

"What if he's not anymore?"

I tense. "You're wrong."

"Your dad needs help, Rebel."

My hands tighten around the gun.

"I'm guessing he doesn't sleep much."

My palms are getting sweaty; I shift my grip.

"I bet he has sudden mood swings and can't be in public too long without getting restless. Not to mention the constant bouts of anger. Am I right?"

My mouth is dry. How does he know all of this?

Karl's head tilts slightly. "Has he ever been diagnosed with PTSD?" I blink without answering, but it must be enough for Karl because he continues, "That's what I thought."

"You don't know how he was before," I say, still feeling the need to defend him.

"You're right," Karl says and then stands next to me. "But these militia groups love guys like your dad. Former military. Police officers with a taste for living on the edge. And what's not to love? It gives them legitimacy since people like your dad already have weapons experience, leadership skills. Your dad's accustomed to following orders and can survive—even thrive—in the worst conditions." He lifts a finger. "But the number one reason I think Wade is going to use your dad: loyalty."

"My dad wouldn't hurt someone just because he's loyal to the Flag Bearers."

"Are you sure about that?"

Outside, a truck's engine rumbles. "I need to go," I say, turning away from him.

"Rebel," he calls. "Stop." There's something about the way he says it that makes me stop. "Even if you don't help me, I'd feel a whole lot better if you'd at least let me get you home to your aunt."

He knows about Aunt Birdie? Suddenly, I'm worried for her. Dad didn't want them to know. "Do the Flag Bearers know about her?"

"No," he says. "Just me."

I shake my head, not sure I can trust him. "You'll send me home even if I don't help you?"

He nods. "This isn't a place for kids. I said so when you first arrived, and I still believe that. Even Wade knows it. He's about to tell his own daughter she can't come with us."

"But how?" My heart flutters with the possibility. "How would you get me home?"

"I'd tell Wade you need to ride with me tonight so we can discuss another weapons order and how fast you can get it together. Then I'll find a way to get you to one of my guys, and we'll get you home." He doesn't blink. "You say the word, and I'll make sure you're safe."

I could go home.

"Rebel," Dad calls from outside the kill house; my head knocks against the plywood.

Karl squeezes my arm, his expression desperate. "If you tell him I'm FBI, he'll kill me. No questions asked."

"I want to go home," I blurt, hearing Dad's approach.

Karl nods and releases me as Dad peeks around the corner.

"I thought you were learning how to shoot in here," Dad says, sounding suspicious.

"He is," Karl says at the same time I say, "I am."

Smooth.

"Haven't heard any gunshots in a while," Dad notes.

"I've been talking him through it. You're kid's a thinker before a doer," Karl explains and then nods to me. "Show him, Rebel."

I eye Karl, surprised. He's figured me out after only knowing me for a little while. Dad still hasn't figured me out, and it's been over thirteen years.

"Let's see it, then," Dad says.

With a breath, I force myself calm and raise the weapon.

"Remember everything I told you," Karl says.

I take another breath and glance through the scope, through the crosshairs toward the front notch, before edging around the corner and outside. I stall a second for my eyes to adjust to the changing light—it's brighter, with the sun filtering between the trees. I keep the gun tight against my shoulder, like Karl said, and line up the notch with my target about a hundred feet away. I hold my breath before I fire. *Boom!*

Immediately, Dad pushes me aside and runs upfield to check. When he gets there, he slaps the target with his hand. "It's a kill," he calls.

"Really?" I ask, my heart galloping.

Karl and I hurry to join him to see where I've struck—a

bit to the right of the heart. "I wouldn't believe it if I didn't see it with my own eyes," Dad says, a huge grin brightening his face.

I smile, too. Not because it's a kill. But because I did that: I made him smile.

"He's a natural," Karl adds.

Dad laughs. "Don't know how you did it, Karl, but you must be some kind of a genius."

Karl nods toward me. "I had a good student."

"This is great," Dad says. "Now you can do more than assembly on our next mission."

My smile falls.

He gestures at the building where I assembled the guns. "Come on, the other kids are already helping, and I need you to clean weapons and get them packed. We have a long drive ahead of us."

TWENTY-TWO

The licorice-like smell of Ballistol hovers in the air. I've been cleaning guns all afternoon in the WHITES ONLY building, trying to think of a way to convince Dad we can't follow the Flag Bearers to Washington, D.C.

The only thing I can come up with? The truth.

I don't want them to hurt Karl, but my dad's greatest fear has come to life: The feds are after him. And I don't want him to get into more trouble than he already is.

Karl doesn't believe me, but I know, deep down, my dad's a good person. He would never intentionally hurt innocent people. I also know if he follows Wade into battle, only trouble will follow.

I *have* to get him alone—tell him about Karl. But I can't seem to get him alone with all of the preparations before the big move.

Disassembled parts of the last gun sit on the table in front of me. I take the firing pin and groan to myself. It feels like this is the thousandth gun I've cleaned, though it's probably more like the sixtieth.

"How's it coming?" Dad asks as he walks into the building and lifts another crate full of clean weapons from the floor.

I sit up, taking my chance. "I need to tell you something."

But then the door flings open; Dwight marches into the building, followed by Justin, and, within earshot, they count the stacked boxes of hand grenades.

Dad looks at me, waiting.

"Almost done." I slump in my chair and spray Ballistol onto the pin in my hand and wipe, graying an old cloth with the carbon deposits I rub off the pin.

"Good," Dad says. "Because, when you're finished here, I need to give you something." His boots clomp against the concrete as he walks away, carrying the full crate outside.

"Pretty exciting stuff, huh?" Justin says, stopping his count to glance over at me.

"Exciting," I say, not feeling at all excited as I spray the retainer pin. What am I going to do?

When I finish cleaning the parts, I reassemble the final gun and carefully place it inside the wooden crate, sealing it with a lid. I struggle to lift the same kind of box Dad lifted easily. I grunt as I carry the crate to the door, nudging it open with my foot.

Outside the building, there's an assembly line of men and kids loading a U-Haul. "I'll take it," one of the guys says, pulling the crate from my hands and placing it in line for the truck. I rub my biceps and take a look inside the cargo space. It's full of enough survival kits, gas masks, and unmarked boxes of weapons to start World War III.

I have to find Dad. I scan the groupings of Flag Bearers when I spot Morgan and Wade, standing next to another U-Haul. She's crying, her face red and snotty.

I slowly walk a little closer and stop, pretending to fiddle with my bootlaces as I crane my neck to hear what on earth could make this girl cry.

"I can't take you with me, sweetie," Wade says, attempting to dry her tears with his scarred hand.

She pushes his hand away and sniffles. "You're going to miss my birthday."

"I know." He pulls her into his arms. "But I'm doing this for you."

"I don't want you to go," she mumbles.

He kisses the top of her head. "Bravery requires selflessness."

She nods and buries her ruddy face in his chest.

"It kind of sucks for her, doesn't it?" Justin says as he approaches from behind.

I pretend to finish tying my laces before I stand. "What?"

He gestures at Morgan. "She's one of the best shooters, and she doesn't even get to go."

So Karl was right: Wade's not letting any of the kids come with us. "Surprises me," I lie.

Justin shakes his head, eyeing me with something like jealousy. "You're the only kid going." Then he puffs his chest. "At least I get to stay and help our dads with the special mission, which is probably more dangerous anyway."

Dangerous? Did he include my dad in that? "Special mission?"

Justin nods, like he's expecting me to be impressed. But I have no idea what he's talking about. "I thought you knew about it," he said.

"Oh, yeah. That," I say, hoping he'll now think I'm the one who's jealous.

He laughs. "Yeah, it's going to be awesome." Justin slaps my arm. "Did you see the blueprints your dad got?"

I shake my head.

"Oh, you should ask him to show them to you. He got them from the city records department so Wade could pinpoint the best places to start the shooting."

Shooting? It feels like an invisible pair of hands is squeezing my throat. I can't speak.

Justin laughs. "He even called the church to figure out what time the service begins—can you believe it?"

I cough, forcing myself to swallow. "Church?"

"Yeah, the place should be full, too." Justin grins. "Remind me never to cross your dad, okay?"

My knees buckle. It can't be. But it's the only thing that fits. There's only one place he could be talking about: Josiah's church.

No, that can't be right. There has to be some kind of mistake. Karl didn't mention anything about a special mission, or a church shooting. He said we're going to Washington, D.C. The mission is there, not here.

My gaze spins around the camp. "Have you seen my dad?" I ask, frantic, searching the men moving around the grounds, the ones finishing with the trucks and saying goodbye to their kids. "He said he needed to give me something."

Justin looks for a moment. "There," he says, pointing at the watchtower on the far side of the clearing. "But you better hurry. Everyone's about to leave."

Dad is already halfway up the ladder, climbing to the top.

I run toward him, jostling between the moving men and kids, the grenades and the guns.

When I reach the ladder, my hands grasp the metal rails. My heart pounds harder as I climb, my boots striking each step with a *bong, bong, bong.*

"Oh, hey, Rebs," Dad says, his voice calm as he leans out the open side window. He disappears and, within seconds, slides open the floor hatch.

From the top of the ladder, I stretch my arms overhead, clutching the sides of the rectangular opening with my fingertips and pull myself into the gray tower. The floor is about the size of four robotics tables smushed together and smells of sawdust.

Dad is on one knee on the plywood floor. He pulls three pairs of binoculars off a low shelf before placing them inside an olive-green knapsack I've never seen before. One of our bug-out bags sits on the floor next to the knapsack.

"You wanted to give me something?" I ask.

He nods as a truck's engine turns, followed by another.

Dad stands, leaving the knapsack on the floor, and looks out the main window of the watchtower. He rubs the stubble along his cheek. "Not much time now."

I near the window.

From our bird's-eye view, I can see the unmarked bus sitting where the training grounds used to be. Morgan is wiping her tears in the front row by herself and, one by one, the other kids salute Wade before boarding the bus.

Dwight stands at attention next to Wade, while Justin is like a statue next to his dad. My stomach takes another turn. What if there really is a "special mission"?

The rest of the men are getting inside their trucks, ready to leave.

"Karl and I have been talking," Dad says, still looking outside. He lifts a hand in a short wave.

My shoulders tighten as I wonder if Dad knows Karl is an FBI agent. Would Dad really kill him? And if he doesn't know, should I tell him so he doesn't get into any more trouble than he already is?

"Talking about what?" I ask as Karl waves back at Dad.

The U-Hauls rumble and disappear along the bumpy road between the trees. Dad inches away from the window and grabs the bug-out bag. "You're going to ride with Karl to our next location."

I shake my head. "I want to be with you."

He hands me the bag. "I put extra packets of dried strawberries in here for the road." He gives me a small smile. "I know how much you like them."

Is he really talking about strawberries at a time like this? "Why can't we ride together?"

"I've been given a special mission," he says.

I drop the bag with a heavy *thud*.

Dad jumps at the sound and begins pacing. He's not looking at me anymore.

"Special mission?"

"I'll need to hang back for a few days."

"But why?" I ask. "What are you going to be doing?"

He stops. "I need you to go ahead with the others, and I'll meet you there when I'm done."

"And what if I say no?"

"Don't be ridiculous," Dad says. He moves over to the same shelf with the binoculars and grabs a flashlight. He clicks it on—making a bright circle of light on the wall—and then off. Seeming satisfied, he lifts the green knapsack from the floor and props it on the windowsill in front of me.

Now's my chance to tell him. *Karl's an FBI agent*, I say in my head, practicing as I open my mouth to tell him.

He drops the flashlight into a loop on the side of the bag; the weight pulls the knapsack open slightly, revealing the corner of something I could swear looks like . . . a blueprint.

No, it can't be.

"What's wrong?" Dad asks.

I blink once, twice, trying to clear my vision when I spot the letters *AME* scribbled in the corner of the wrinkled paper. My heart stops.

Dad seems to follow my gaze and immediately cinches the knapsack closed before I can read the rest.

Wasn't Josiah's church called the "AME Zion Church"?

"Rebel?" Dad asks.

I wipe my hands on my pants, staring at Dad's hardened face. Karl was right: He isn't a hero anymore. Not if he's planning to attack a church full of innocent people. I think of Calliope and snatch my bug-out bag.

"You okay? You look like you've seen a ghost."

I nod, biting the inside of my cheek and forcing back the tears. "I've got to—go," I mumble before slinging the bug-out bag over my shoulder and hurrying to the hole in the floor. My foot reaches for the ladder.

"Wait," Dad orders, and for some reason, my body still obeys. My foot comes off the ladder as he slowly approaches. To my surprise, he immediately pulls me against his strong chest. "Too old to give me a hug now?"

My arms mechanically swing around him; I breathe in his familiar woodsy scent. Wrapped inside his strong arms, I feel like a little boy again.

I could still tell him. I could still save him from his own hate.

But if I do, can I really trust he won't hurt Karl? And even if he's willing to leave right now, would he call off the special mission? Could I trust Wade and Dwight to leave Josiah and Calliope alone? Could I really stop their hate?

Dad squeezes me tight. "Who watches the watchmen?"

Disappointment floods every part of me. I quickly pull away and answer, "You do."

TWENTY-THREE

Dad closes my door and stands next to Karl's truck, an assault rifle slung around his front. He didn't hug me again, but now he gives me a slight wave. The engine rumbles. Or maybe the wave was for Karl.

I roll down the passenger window. "Bye."

"See you in a few days," Dad says before turning the opposite direction.

My insides churn, knowing what he plans to do between now and then.

Leaves and branches crunch beneath the tires as Karl drives us toward the narrow road between the trees. I spot Dad's reflection in the truck's side-view mirror. He's talking with Wade and Dwight and Justin. Probably about their special mission. I feel like I'm going to be sick.

We hit the first rut; the truck's shocks squeak. "Ready to see your aunt?" Karl asks.

I wipe the sweat from my forehead.

"We're going into town first thing. There's an officer there, ready to take you to Amarillo."

Home. I could go home.

I roll up the window, sealing out the smell of dirt and trees.

"This time tomorrow, you'll be in your own room."

It would be so easy to go. I could keep all the thoughts inside my head like always. I could go home and forget about the paranoia and guns and hate. But what about Josiah? Calliope?

Karl nudges my arm as we go over another bump. "You okay, kid?" He returns his hand to the wheel so he can maneuver through the trees.

I could nod. He wouldn't ask me again. I could go home. I could forget.

We bounce in another trench; the engine groans. But I know I couldn't forget her. Not really. I don't want to forget.

I swallow hard before speaking. "I know what they're planning." It comes out louder than I expect.

Karl's eyes are on me, instead of the road where they should be.

"Tree!" I yell, pointing.

He jerks the wheel left, barely avoiding the wide trunk. The tree's branches scratch the right side of his truck. When we're clear, he nods. "Go on," he says, keeping his eyes forward.

"It's not what you think."

"What?"

"The mission," I say and then shake my head. "It is, but it isn't."

Karl shifts in his seat. I can sense him tensing next to me. "You're going to have to help me out here."

I release a hard sigh, frustrated. Why am I so bad at this?

"Why don't you start from the beginning?" he reasons. "Baby steps."

"Okay," I say and try to breathe, but it's hard with all the bumps and ruts. I grab hold of the overhead bar. "There's a special mission."

"In Washington?"

"No," I say, shaking my head. "Yes, there is a mission there. But there's another one."

"Where?"

"Here," I say and then correct myself, "In Mercy." I take another breath. "They're planning to attack Josiah's church. They've got blueprints. And guns. And probably bombs," I say, the faucet of words opening wider with each confession.

"We have to stop them. We have to tell Calliope. We can't let them die. We—"

"Slow down," Karl says, his voice steady. "Do you know when?"

We bounce; my fingers slip from the grab bar. "Tomorrow."

"Dammit," Karl says. "I'm sorry, but that's awfully fast."

"I know," I say, my voice jittery. My hands are shaking. "After they attack the church, they're meeting with the others in Washington for their next mission."

And suddenly, we're out of the trees. Our tires run along the smooth pavement for a minute before Karl pulls over to the side of the road. "Are you sure you didn't misunderstand?" he asks, monitoring his rearview mirror. "Because this is the first I've heard of an attack on a church."

My fingernails dig into his cloth seat. He doesn't believe me. "You asked me to help you, and I am. You told me yourself Wade was paranoid, and he only tells those who are involved in the mission."

Karl seems to consider me for a second and then straightens behind the wheel. "I don't want to redirect resources when we should be focusing on Washington."

"Can't you focus on both? I thought you worked for the FBI."

The muscle below Karl's right eye twitches. He faces

forward again, dropping the gearshift. "I'll take you into town," he says, checking one more time before he pulls onto the empty road. "I'll make some calls." We move along the switchbacks, swaying down the mountain.

I don't think he believes me. "What about Josiah and Calliope? What about the church? We can't leave them. We have to warn them."

"There's no *we*. You're going home," he says and nods. "Don't worry, I'll take care of it."

"But they won't trust you," I say, shifting in my seat to face him. I'm not sure I completely trust him. I pull the seat belt from my throat. "You saw how Calliope reacted when she saw you coming." Even though I know he's FBI, he still looks like one of them. "She thinks you're one of them."

"What are you suggesting?"

"Let me tell them."

"*You?*" he says with a laugh.

But I'm not laughing.

"Forget it. You're going home."

Heat flashes along my skin. "You forget it," I say, my voice rising. "You're too busy worrying about whatever's happening in Washington to worry about my friends. If you don't tell them, I will. I'll jump from this truck and run back if I have to."

Karl shoots me a hard look. "You don't understand."

"I understand plenty," I say, every muscle tightening. "There's not much time, you said so yourself."

We sway across the final switchback; Karl releases a long sigh. "You know what, kid? I think I liked it better when you didn't talk so much."

***

My boots move swiftly, brushing through the red flowers. "There," I say, pointing to Josiah and Calliope's cabin. The logs glow like amber in the fading sunlight. I glance over my shoulder at Karl. His face is focused, scary. "We still look like them. We probably should've changed clothes first."

"No time, remember?" he says dryly. We couldn't go through camp, or the Flag Bearers would see us, so we had to take the long way to their cabin. All the way over, Karl was calling and trying to gather area law enforcement, trying to convince them a kid was a trustworthy informant. I wanted to ask him how he got such good service out here but figured it was an FBI thing.

We hurry up the ramps, our heavy boots thumping all the way to the porch. I stop in front of the wide red door.

Karl gestures. "Aren't you going to knock?" he says, impatiently standing behind me. "You're the one who *had* to come, remember?"

My knuckles strike the door. Once. Twice. Three times.

"Who's there?" Calliope asks.

I can hear her approaching footfalls. "Me," I answer, trying to keep my voice from sounding strange.

She swings the door open, wearing her soccer clothes and a smile. And then she sees who's standing behind me. Her smile immediately disappears; her eyes go wide with fear.

"Please," I say, holding up a hand. "Wait."

The door starts swinging; Karl lodges his foot in the threshold so she can't close it.

She backs away.

Tires squeak against the floor as Josiah rolls into the room. "Who is it, Peanut?"

Calliope grabs his wheelchair. "He led them here," she says, looking at me.

I hurry inside, shaking my head. "It's not what you think."

"I'm with the FBI," Karl says, strolling in behind me. He flashes a badge, so cheesy, like they do in the movies.

Calliope looks skeptical, and I don't blame her.

"He's an undercover agent," I hurry to explain. "He's been living with the Flag Bearers for several months, building a case against them."

Her eyes narrow with disbelief, like I told her Karl is the long-lost descendant of the tooth fairy.

Josiah gently touches Calliope's hand, signaling her to

release his chair. He rolls it forward. "I'm sorry, but I don't understand what any of this has to do with us."

Karl puts his badge away. "We have reason to believe your church is the subject of a planned attack."

"Attack?" Calliope says.

Josiah gestures to the plaid sofa. "Please."

"Thank you," Karl says and then sits.

I edge toward the stone fireplace. Too anxious to sit, I stand next to the mantel. Calliope moves to the other side.

With all of us facing one another, Karl continues, "Our informant tells us it's scheduled for tomorrow's service."

Josiah squeezes the arms of his wheelchair. "So soon?"

"I'm sorry," Karl says. "We came as soon as we found out."

"You told him," Calliope deducts, staring at me, seeing right through me. "That's why you're here, isn't it?"

I nod.

"How long have you known?"

"I didn't know until a few hours ago."

She looks like she's trying to decide whether to believe me or not.

"Rebel insisted we come warn you first," Karl says, an edge of irritation to his voice.

"Grab my directory," Josiah says with a new sense of urgency. "We need to go into town and call the congregation.

They need to know they shouldn't come to church tomorrow."

"I think that would be best," Karl says.

Calliope shakes her head. "But those guys will get away."

"Ma'am," Karl says, "let us do our jobs. This is for your own safety."

"Don't ma'am me," Calliope snaps. She's looking straight at Karl.

I bite down a smile.

"I may be just a kid, but I'm not so naive as to believe if they aren't arrested, they'll pack their guns and go home."

"She's right," I say, facing her. "They're planning to attack Washington next."

From the corner of my eye, I see Karl's hand twist the cushion like he's imagining it's me. "Rebel, that's supposed to be classified."

"They're planning to attack our nation's capital?" Josiah asks, concern lining his voice.

"No," Karl says at the same time I say, "Yes." Karl shakes his head.

"Well, which is it?" Josiah asks.

Karl leans against the cushion and sighs. "The plan is, after they hit your church, they will be joining a larger militia in order to attack Washington, D.C." He locks his fingers together. "I'm sorry, but that's all I can tell you; you've already heard too much." He glares at me.

"If we cancel the service," Josiah says, "do you think they will still try to damage the building?"

"I think once they see the church is empty, they'll move on. This is probably more of a—" Karl clears his throat "—more of a personal matter."

"Because of me, right?" I say. "Because they're my friends."

"It's true your dad wasn't happy with your choice of friends." Karl glances at Calliope.

Her jaw tightens.

"But the real reason here is racism. It's hate—plain and simple." He purses his lips and then turns to Josiah. "Why don't we take you into town so you can call your members? I need to meet up with some of my folks once we get there. But you can start making calls on my phone on the drive over."

Josiah nods and reaches for the wheels of his chair.

Calliope places a hand on his shoulder, stopping him. "But what's to guarantee they won't come another time? Who's to say tomorrow will be the end of it?"

"They won't come back," Karl says, confident. "We'll catch them in Washington and—"

"But what if you don't?" I press. "I'm sorry, but I've found out in a few weeks what you couldn't find out in nine months."

His face flushes red.

"What if we still have tomorrow's service?" Calliope asks.

"Forget it," Karl says. "That's a no go."

"But why?" she asks. "We can lure them in—stop them now—before they leave town."

Karl stands. "I don't think you two understand: This isn't some game. We're talking about real guns here and men who know how to use them."

"I'm not willing to put my congregation in danger," Josiah adds, shaking his head. "But, God knows, I would like to keep these men from hurting anyone."

"I can't guarantee your safety." Karl's hand slices the air. "I'm not going to endanger civilians for the chance we *might* catch them."

I step toward him. "But what if you catch them here and they can tell you the plan for Washington? It might give you a few extra days to get your people together and stop them there."

Karl dismisses my words with his hand. "You don't know if these guys have information about the planned attack."

"And you don't know that they don't," I reason.

"Would anybody care to ask what we want to do?" Calliope says.

She's right: Nobody's asked. "What do you want?" I say.

She lifts her chin. "I *want* us to stand our ground."

Karl scoffs. "Have you seen what a gun can do?"

"Yes," I say, willing my voice to remain strong. "And I think she's right. This is your best chance of stopping the attacks, and you know it."

Karl turns to Josiah. "Will you *please* talk some sense into them? These kids think they can take on one of the best-armed militias in the country." He points his finger at me. "This isn't a game, Rebel. You've seen these men. If you interfere, your dad won't care that you're his son."

"But *I* can still care that he's my dad," I say. "And I don't want him to hurt anyone else."

Josiah melds his hands together like he's praying. "'To ignore evil is to become an accomplice to it.'"

Calliope smiles. "Dr. Martin Luther King, Jr. said that."

Josiah nods; I nod.

Karl looks between us. "Alright, then. What do you suggest?"

TWENTY-FOUR

I shift my weight on the folding chair at the back of the room, this time moving from hunched over to sitting up. My knee bobs up and down with nerves as Josiah preaches.

He holds a Bible and sits front and center, speaking into a microphone: "If we are to loosen the bonds of hate, we must come together. We must go beyond simply calling ourselves neighbors. We must act like neighbors. Break bread together. Visit one another's homes. Truly get to know one another. Only then can we see our shared humanity."

At this moment over in Mercy, undercover agents are pretending to be the congregation of the AME Zion Church, trying to lure and trap the Flag Bearers.

But we are the *real* congregation. We sit together in a makeshift church one county away. Black people. Brown people. White people.

Heads nod as Josiah preaches. A few people shout, "Amen!"

This is how Josiah stands his ground. Not by directly facing the Flag Bearers' attack—he insisted that's the job of the FBI now—but by bringing people together.

While Karl scrambled to gather a team of federal and local law enforcement, Josiah and Calliope called church members, instructing them not to come to the usual building today. They also called pastors and friends from other area churches, from schools, and from soccer teams. Less than twenty-four hours later, this community center was *the* place to gather instead.

We sit shoulder to shoulder now, the massive room full. The smell of home-cooked food surrounds us, literally crammed on tables around the room, for the potluck lunch planned following the service.

I glance sideways at the clock above the metal double doors. It's almost noon. My neck tightens. We should've heard something by now.

What if the Flag Bearers don't surrender? What if Dad doesn't?

"You alright?" Calliope asks under her breath. She sits to my right, wearing a pretty yellow dress.

I wipe my hands on my jeans and nod.

"Liar," she whispers with a coy smile.

My cheeks heat.

"I'm sure he's fine," she says and then takes my hand. Calliope's warm fingers wrap around mine, sending a thousand jolts of electricity throughout my body.

For a split second, I wonder if she'll remember how I almost didn't speak up. How I failed to speak up so many times before. What if she reconsiders? I hold my breath, waiting. My heart beats with worry. With hope.

Josiah closes his Bible and points to the projection screen on the wall behind him. A slide pops up with what looks like song lyrics. "Now, if you will rise in body or in spirit and join me in singing our closing hymn: 'This Little Light of Mine.'"

The chairs creak as almost everyone stands. From the front of the room, a woman pounds out notes on an upright piano that sits beneath the screen. A man joins Josiah and lifts the microphone from the stand. He starts to sing with a deep, full voice:

> *"This little light of mine,*
> *I'm going to let it shine."*

The congregation repeats the verse. Old voices join young ones. Chills race along my arms. The man sings it again and so does the congregation. It's so beautiful. People start clapping to the beat and, by the end of the first verse, the whole congregation sways side to side as they sing. Everyone, including me, is smiling. Singing loudly. Even the people who can't sing do at the top of their lungs. It doesn't matter.

For a split second, I'm only thinking about the music and these people who look nothing alike—the tune moving through all of us like a single instrument.

Calliope suddenly nudges me with her elbow and then points toward the double doors. I freeze in place. Karl is there, holding one of the doors open. His eyes search the congregation until they finally land on me.

"Go," Calliope says with a reassuring nod.

As everyone starts the third verse, I rush behind our row of chairs and around the side of the room, careful not to bump into the food tables.

"Let's talk out here," Karl says when I reach him. And by the way he says it—stiff and flat—I know something's wrong.

I swallow hard and follow him into the quiet, empty hallway. Too quiet. The fluorescents buzz overhead and flicker at random as Karl carefully closes the door, shutting out the beautiful music with a *click*.

"It's done," Karl says.

I give a swift nod, wanting him to hurry up and tell me *what* is done. My dad? Josiah's church?

Karl runs a hand across the side of his head. He won't look at me.

This is bad. My fingernails dig into the meat of my hand.

"We got them," Karl says. He glances at his watch. He's still not looking at me.

Got them. What does that mean?

He glances over my shoulder. "Wade, Dwight, and Justin approached from the rear of the church, but we surrounded them pretty quickly. They surrendered without incident." Karl clears his throat.

My heart thrums loudly.

"Your dad tried to enter through the front of the church."

"He tried?" I take in a sharp breath, bracing for the worst.

Karl places a steadying hand on my shoulder and looks me straight in the eye. "He's alive, Rebel."

Air escapes my chest. "He is?"

Karl nods. "Nathan didn't want to surrender. It wasn't easy." His hand falls from my shoulder. "It took four agents to subdue him."

Subdue him?

"But we finally got him safely into custody."

"Thank you," I say, a mix of feelings swirling inside.

"This is a good thing," Karl says before dryly laughing to himself. "We think Dwight and Justin will probably talk to save their skins."

"And my dad?" I ask, daring to hope. "Do you think he'll help, too?"

Karl's expression tightens. "Honestly, no."

My shoulders sink with disappointment, even though I know he's probably right.

"But hey, if you hadn't told us about their plans, there could've been a lot of innocent people hurt today, or worse." He points toward the closed doors. "You saved them."

I shake my head, thinking of Josiah's wisdom. Calliope's courage. And how all these people came together to take a stand against hate. "I think they saved me."

"Or you saved yourself," Karl says with a wink.

My face flushes hot. "Maybe a little of both."

"Yeah, maybe," Karl says and then glances at his watch with a sigh. "I still need to fill out a ton of paperwork, but I wanted you to hear it from me: Your father may finally get the help he needs."

"That would be good," I note, trying to sound more confident than I feel. I've heard that before.

He thumbs toward the other room. "Sounds like they're wrapping up in there."

I can hear Josiah over the speakers, talking about "next time."

"Enjoy lunch, and I'll be back in a few hours to take you home."

"You?" I ask.

"Don't act so surprised." Karl grins smugly. "I actually requested the assignment."

"You're serious?"

"You did good, kid," he says, clicking his heels to attention. To my surprise, he salutes me.

I don't know how to respond; I awkwardly salute him back.

With a confident nod, Karl turns to walk away, calling over his shoulder, "Don't forget to save me some pie."

When he's gone, a strange combination of relief and sadness tumbles my insides. No one was hurt. Josiah's church is safe. My dad is in jail.

Happy chatter and the sounds of tables and chairs being dragged across the floor suddenly grow louder. I catch a whiff of lemons and honey. "Calliope," I say, turning to face her in the open doorway.

"Are you okay?" she asks as soon as she sees my face. A line of concern runs across her forehead; she shuts the metal door behind her, muffling the noise.

"Yes," I answer because it's easiest.

She looks like she doesn't believe me. "Did the FBI catch them?"

"Yes," I say again and, before I can stop myself, I reach out to her.

Calliope comes closer until our fingertips touch, making my stomach flutter. "You sure you're okay?"

I nod out of habit and then look into her dark and searching eyes, deciding to finally answer honestly instead. I shake my head. "Yes and no."

She smiles, her fingers fully lacing through mine. "Did you know Charles Darwin was one of the first scientists to write about emotions in animals?"

I laugh a little. Here we go again.

"And feelings of optimism have been shown in a wide variety of species besides humans."

A grin tugs at my lips. "I did not know that."

"It's true," she says. "Even honeybees have feelings." Without warning, she leans in, kissing me softly on the cheek.

My chest fills with warmth, like sunshine on a summer day. "What was that for?"

Calliope's smile brightens. "You finally found your voice."

TWENTY-FIVE

Three Months Later

Our kitchen smells like warm bread. Aunt Birdie opens the oven to retrieve the biscuits; I quickly pull N8TE 2.0 to the edge of the table for one more test run. With the gray arrows, I move through the programs and select the one I want before pressing start.

N8TE rolls away from my hands, past the butter and jelly, to the stack of sugar packets. I built this robot off the design I'd first imagined in the cabin, with some improvements. N8TE comes to a stop and sorts the packets, flipping half of them label side up with the other half label side down. At the same time, the arm on the other side of the cage is cranking as if moving the wheel that will be on the actual competition board.

"So you have it doing two things at once now?" Aunt Birdie slides a platter of hot biscuits onto the table.

I nod. "Hopefully, it will save some time and give me more design points."

"Impressive," she says with a smile. "Should I tell them to hand you the championship trophy when we get there or make everyone suffer through the competition first?"

I smile a little and then shake my head. "There are a lot of other kids who are just as good. Better even," I say, thinking of one.

She winks and turns to open the refrigerator.

N8TE completes the tasks and rolls to the starting point in front of me. I shift in my seat. This afternoon is the Fall Robotics Showcase and the first time I'll see Ajeet since I spray-painted his locker. "Besides, the judges might not take me seriously."

"Why wouldn't they?" Aunt Birdie asks, pushing the refrigerator door closed with her hip.

"Because my new school doesn't have a robotics program."

There are three conditions I had to meet for me to return to school after getting expelled last spring. One, I have to go to a completely different school. Two, I was supposed to write a letter of apology to my old principal, Mrs. Fuentes, which

I already did. And three, I have to take anger management classes for a year. I expected the first two, but the third one really annoyed me.

Aunt Birdie said I haven't had the best role models when it comes to seeking help, and that's exactly why I need it. And she's right.

Therapy was really, *really* hard at first, but it seems to be getting easier. I don't feel so knotted-up inside, and I'm starting to learn how to control my anger before it controls me.

She sets a glass of orange juice in front of me. "Once they see your robot in action, they won't have much of a choice but to take you seriously." She gestures for me to clear the table. "Time for breakfast."

I nestle N8TE in my hands, move over to the bench, and lower him into the crate. I can't help but think how empty the floor looks without Dad's bug-out bags lined beneath the bench.

"What time are Calliope and Josiah coming again?" Aunt Birdie asks.

I smile to myself. Calliope and I have kept in touch like old-fashioned pen pals. Since she doesn't have a phone, it's been the only way to talk to her. It's a little slow—okay, *painfully* slow—but it works. "Around noon."

"It's nice of them to spend their weekend on the road to come cheer you on today." She clears her throat. "I get the feeling this Calliope may be more than a friend?"

I shake my head. "I've already told you: I don't know what you're talking about."

"Mmm-hmmm," she says and then taps the newspaper with a finger, her face turning serious. "Did you see this morning's paper?"

I move to the table and read the headline: SIX MORE ARRESTS IN PLANNED ATTACK ON NATION'S CAPITOL. My neck tightens. After Dad was arrested, the FBI questioned everyone they'd caught. Justin said he didn't know anything. Wade and Dad refused to answer their questions. Dwight, however, wasn't so loyal. Faced with prison, Dwight talked in exchange for a lighter sentence and revealed the Flag Bearers' plans for a full-scale attack with help from other militia groups around the country. I didn't realize there were so many of them until the newspaper spelled it all out in black and white.

"Do you want to talk about it?" Aunt Birdie asks.

I force myself to take a deep breath and exhale. "Maybe later," I say before taking a biscuit from the platter.

She cuts a biscuit in half and carves a pat of butter from

the stick, plopping it between the two halves. "I got another letter from him," she says, setting the biscuit on her dish, letting the butter melt.

My gut twists as Aunt Birdie pulls a crumpled envelope from the pocket of her sweater. She removes the trifold pages from the envelope, marked with Dad's chicken-scratch handwriting. "The judge has ordered him to undergo therapy for PTSD."

I don't look at her, afraid of what my eyes might reveal: doubt. "What did he think?" I stare straight at the globs of purple jelly stuck inside the glass jar.

She sighs. "He doesn't want to go to therapy, but he does want you to visit."

Heat surges through my fingers. The biscuit crumbles between them. I immediately brush the crumbs into my cupped hand. "Sorry," I say before dropping them onto my plate.

"No worries." Within seconds, Aunt Birdie places a new biscuit on my plate. "There's something else."

"What?" I ask, taking the warm bread.

She glances at the biscuit in my hand.

I set it on the plate and take a breath. "What did he say?"

Aunt Birdie draws a smaller, sealed envelope from inside

the folds of the letter. "He wrote to you, too." She offers it to me, and when I don't take it, she places it next to my plate on top of a few stray crumbs.

I press my lips together. I don't want to read it, but I do. It's all I can do to keep my hands from shaking.

Slowly, I rip the flap from the envelope and remove the paper inside. One sheet. Two sentences:

I'm sorry. Can you forgive me?

That's it? It's a little too complicated for "I'm sorry" now. Anger flashes through me. *Forgive you for what exactly? There's so much to forgive.* Followed by cold fear. *What if he never changes? What if the only way I can see him again is behind bars?* And finally, the numb of sadness. *Why did he do this to us?*

Aunt Birdie's hand covers mine. "Are you okay?" Her eyes probe gently. "Are you ready to visit him?"

I know she wants me to tell her I'd love to see my dad. That I'm ready to take the next step. But the truth is, I don't know right now. My feelings are all jumbled inside. I don't want to see him in that place. I love him, but I don't really like him. And I'm not sure if I can ever forgive him.

So I open my mouth, and that's exactly what I say.

***

Calliope and I walk behind Josiah's wheelchair, with Aunt Birdie beside him. I was a little nervous about Josiah and Aunt Birdie not having anything in common. Apparently, I was worried about nothing.

Both of them have the gift—or curse, depending on how you look at it—of being able to talk to anybody, anytime, for as long as they like. They've spanned topics ranging from car repair to Crock-Pot recipes, from politics (thankfully, they agree) to the difficulty of raising teens. Calliope and I roll our eyes on the last one.

My muscles tighten as we approach the gym of my old school. Since Ajeet is last year's Regionals champion, the showcase is held here to start the season. I had to get special permission to even be here.

We cross into the gym. "So, *this* is the Nerd Den," Calliope jokes.

"Hey," I say carefully nudging her with my elbow. I don't want to drop N8TE or my spare-parts crate. "I'd like to remind you that you're the one who drove several hundred miles to visit this nerd." I nod at the She-Hulk T-shirt she's wearing. It was in the last package I sent to her. "Obviously, you knew what you were getting into when you met me."

She smiles a little. "True."

I find an empty table along the side of the gym—under the basketball goal—and set down my stuff.

"We'll be right there if you need us," Aunt Birdie says, pointing to the stands and then, out of nowhere, she hugs me.

I stiffen, feeling my face turn a dozen shades of red. "Not in front of everyone," I say under my breath.

"Sorry." Immediately, she releases me with a smile, which means she really isn't sorry.

Josiah gives me a thumbs-up. "Go get 'em," he says before they move toward the stands, continuing their conversation about how we're standing on an old prairie dog graveyard.

Calliope sneers. "Well, that was basically awful."

"Tell me about it," I say, watching them get situated on the front row, right in front of the competition table. Great.

"So who's your fiercest competitor? Maybe I can 'accidentally' knock their robot onto the gym floor." She puts accidentally in air quotes.

"You wouldn't."

She shrugs and then breaks into a laugh. "Of course not. Do you really think I'd do something like that?" I open my mouth to answer, but she raises a hand. "Never mind. Don't answer."

Sudden laughter draws my attention across the gym. A

bunch of kids huddle around a guy who seems to be their ringleader. My mouth forms an O. It's Ajeet.

He's taller than the last time I saw him, with the slightest hint of a mustache. The group fawns over him and his robot. They're all joking and laughing. And I should be right there, laughing with them.

"Who's that?" Calliope asks.

I swallow hard. "Ajeet."

Her eyes widen with recognition. "You should go talk to him."

"What?" I ask, turning to her. "Are you crazy?"

"First off, that's not nice," she says, counting off on her fingers. "And second, you'll probably feel better if you get it over with."

"I'm not so sure." I wipe my hands on my jeans. "I mean, what if he won't let me?"

"At least you know you tried." She takes my hand, and I hope it's not too gross and sweaty. "Besides, I thought you were a lot more confident about speaking up now."

"Yeah, but this is different." It was one thing to talk to the FBI. To the police. To Aunt Birdie. Ajeet is a whole other story.

"Ajeet!" Calliope shouts.

My head whips around. "What are you doing?"

"Helping you."

All of a sudden, I can feel him looking.

Calliope lets go and nudges me forward. "I'll be right here when you're done."

I knead my clammy hands and, for a split second, debate running away and never coming back. But I've already run away once, and that didn't turn out so well. I force myself to meet his eyes and move. Each inch feels like a thousand miles in slow motion. It seems like everyone's watching.

The crowd parts around him as I near. "Can I talk to you?" I ask, my voice weaker than I'd like.

From out of nowhere, Mrs. Fuentes slips in front of Ajeet. "Mr. Mercer, I think you need to return to your table."

I nod and turn to walk away.

"No, wait," Ajeet says, or at least I think it's him. His voice is deeper now.

"Are you sure?" Mrs. Fuentes asks.

He nods.

A guy I don't know points at the competition table. "We'll be over here if you need us."

It stings a little to know this guy is probably his best friend now, but I also know it's nobody's fault but mine.

"Thanks," Ajeet says.

When we're alone, I shove my hands inside my jeans pockets, picking at the lint. "Hey."

"Hey," he says, looking everywhere but at me.

"Ajeet," I say and then make myself speak louder. "I wanted to say I'm sorry."

Suddenly, he looks at me, but he doesn't seem too happy. "Is that right?"

I nod. "What I did to you was awful. It was wrong, and I wanted to let you know how sorry I am."

He folds his arms over his chest.

This sucks, but I keep going anyway. "I'd like to be friends again, I mean if you want to." I rock between my feet. "Do you think you could forgive me?"

"You were my friend," he whispers, his lip quivering a little. "But then I saw how much you hated me."

I shake my head. "I *never* hated you. I was angry. I took it out on you, but I never hated you."

Ajeet examines me for a second, like an adult does when he's trying to decide whether to punish me or forgive me.

I hold my breath, waiting.

Finally, he shakes his head. "I'm not really sure I can."

I exhale. The old me would have bitten back. Jumped down his throat. But like me, Ajeet has every right not to forgive. "I understand," I say, even though it hurts.

"So what's with the girl?" he asks with a sudden mischievous grin.

"Calliope?" I ask, turning to look. As promised, she's standing in the same spot. She waves.

He nods like he's impressed. "Maybe you could introduce me to her after I win today."

I laugh a little. "Good luck with your run."

"You too."

I turn to walk toward Calliope.

"Hey, Rebel," Ajeet calls, stopping me. I glance over my shoulder. "You better bring it today," he says, sounding more like his old self. "You have no *idea* what you're up against."

I smile and nod.

"Well?" Calliope asks expectantly as I reach her. "What did he say?"

"Maybe," I say with a slight shrug.

Her enthusiasm fades a little. "It's a start."

There's a tap on the microphone. It echoes throughout the gym before a man welcomes everyone to the competition, urging the teams to their tables in order to get the robots ready.

Since I don't have teammates, Calliope stands with me, helping me keep my nerves in check by asking questions and commenting with random trivia as the other competitors take their turns.

After half of the runs are complete, Ajeet holds the lead with a score that will be tough to beat. But not impossible. If N8TE does everything he's been programmed to do in the given time, I still have a chance to win.

"Rebel Mercer," the judge calls over the noise of the crowd. He gestures to the starting point at the far corner of the table.

Calliope gives my hand a hurried squeeze. "You can do it."

I lift my robot and crate. Alone, I travel the length of the floor to the competition table.

The gym goes silent. The competitors who have already had their turns crowd the table, including Ajeet on the far end.

My heart beats fast as I set N8TE on the starting point and place my spare-parts crate on the floor.

"Go, Rebel!" Calliope and Aunt Birdie shout from their separate places in the gym. My name seems to reverberate forever until Josiah tucks his fingers inside his mouth and whistles loudly. There are a few chuckles around the table, and I'm a little embarrassed. But mostly, I'm glad they're here.

"Ready?" the judge asks.

I turn on N8TE. The red light flashes and then goes steady. The battery is full.

My hands squeeze and relax before I press the arrows, selecting the first program. I nod in response.

"Three, two, one."

With a deep breath, I press the start button and let him go.

Author's Note

Two major issues inspired me to write *The Inside Battle*: (1) certain groups trying to normalize racism in the United States, and (2) our country's ongoing disservice to veterans who suffer from post-traumatic stress disorder (PTSD).

Leading up to and following the 2016 presidential election, I noticed a growing trend toward overt racism. I live in a large, multicultural city with friends from different ethnic backgrounds where explicit racism was something that had always seemed to be happening "someplace else."

To be clear, I was never naive enough to believe we lived in a society where racism was extinct. Even though we were not wealthy growing up, I was aware of the privileges children like me had, ones that other kids my age could only dream of, simply because of my white skin. Raised in a segregated community largely fueled by educational and economic disparity, I heard the racist comments and saw the effects of discrimination. Like Rebel, even though I knew what some people around me were saying or doing was wrong, I felt torn about speaking out against them. After all, weren't some of them the very people I'd been taught to respect and love? Even then, would my voice make a difference?

As I wrestled with these underlying questions from my childhood, I began to research the overarching social issues in this book, starting with the rise of hate groups in our country. Rebel's story is a work of fiction but was inspired, in part, by the growing anti-government movement in the U.S. This trend experienced a comeback in 2008, when President Barack Obama was elected to office, and has only grown since then. These anti-government groups include militias, and though not all militias are racist, many of them are.

Militias typically target former members of the military and law enforcement to join their ranks, due largely to their existing leadership skills, discipline, and weapons experience. Those enlisted by militias are often disgruntled with the government and sometimes suffer from PTSD.

This last fact struck a chord with me since my grandfather suffered from PTSD, though I only realized it later when I grew up and he was no longer with us. We didn't talk about it, which unfortunately isn't all that surprising. As a nation, we freely discuss the sacrifices our soldiers make to ensure our country's freedoms, but we often fail to include the mental health sacrifices they have made alongside the physical ones.

Despite the large numbers of people who suffer from PTSD, the stigma in seeking mental health services remains, particularly for veterans. Soldiers are trained that fear is not tolerated in combat. So when they return home and experience it like Rebel's dad, they are often embarrassed and feel defective, or view themselves as a "coward." Many times, veterans find it challenging to return to their old lives or assimilate into "normal" life.

As I wrestled with these larger issues of our country's ongoing racism and disservice to veterans with PTSD, the underlying question of whether a child's opposing voice could make a difference continually resurfaced. Thankfully, from the time I was very young, my mother encouraged me to speak up, even if my opinion wasn't popular. She taught me that my voice was needed and that I had a right to be heard, though I'm ashamed to admit I didn't always say something when I know I should have. My mother was also the first person to teach me that our population's vast differences (racial, religious, cultural, and so on) are what make our country great. She believed, and continues to believe, that we should always listen and learn from one another.

I have tried to do that. I try to listen, even when it is challenging. I try to understand. I have learned that subtle racism is often more dangerous than overt racism. In listening, I have found that even my multicultural city rests on an undercurrent of racial discrimination. I have discovered that refusing to talk about things, like PTSD, does not mean we are brave. Rather, it takes more courage to say something that makes us vulnerable than it is to remain silent. Finally, I have learned there are opportunities to speak up and call out those who aren't using their privilege for the betterment of humanity as a whole.

My voice matters. The voices of people who aren't like me also matter. Our veterans' voices matter. Your voice does, too, regardless of your age. As Josiah says, *The voices of children matter, especially since they are often the only carriers of truth.*

So, like Rebel, I urge you to find your voice. Use it. Speak up for what is right. Encourage others to do the same. If you don't, who will?

Traumatic experiences, such as war, can have a painful and lasting effect on those who experience it. To learn more about how you can help support our veterans, visit

cnn.com/2013/11/05/us/iyw-simple-ways-to-honor-veterans/index.html

ptsd.va.gov/family/effect_parent_ptsd.asp

giveanhour.org

operationwearehere.com/ChildrenBooksWoundedWarriors.html

Acknowledgments

Writing a book is an isolating process, but I'm so lucky to have a team of people who supported me along the way.

First, I would like to thank my insightful editor, Sonali Fry, for loving Rebel's story, for her honesty when something didn't feel true to the narrative, and for giving me the freedom to find my own solutions. Thank you also to Courtney Fahy for taking the baton with enthusiasm and running alongside me as we brought this book across the finish line.

Thank you to the entire Yellow Jacket crew and the Simon & Schuster sales team for your unending creativity and support of my books. A special note of thanks to Nadia Almahdi, Paul Crichton, Mike Ploetz, Jordan Mondell, and Matthew Sciarappa for working your magic on a daily basis.

I have been so blessed with amazing book covers and that wouldn't have been possible without the talented designer David DeWitt. Thank you, David, for your beautiful work. And thanks to Daniel Zender, who created the powerful artwork that enriches the cover of this book.

Thank you to my agent, Rick Richter, for your initial excitement when I mentioned I was thinking about writing a story about the militia movement and veterans with PTSD.

Your enthusiasm and trust gave me the early push I needed to write this book.

To my amazing critique group, Hema Penmetsa, Polly Holyoke, Pam McWilliams, Robert Eilers, and Laney Nielson, thank you! Your feedback was essential, and I'm so grateful for your continued encouragement and camaraderie on this writing journey.

When I started, I knew I had to learn about guns, something that, like Rebel, made me incredibly nervous. Thank you to my friend and Gulf War veteran, Kevin O'Brien, for taking me to the gun range, teaching me how to safely fire different kinds of weapons, and answering all of my questions. I'm thankful for your expertise, patience, and especially your kindness. Any errors in this book regarding weapons are mine and mine alone.

And thank you to Cynthia O'Brien for your friendship and enthusiastic support of my books. Your presence at the gun range made me far less nervous than I would have otherwise been. A wholehearted thanks for the laughs that kept me from breaking down in tears that day. You're the best!

A HUGE thank-you to all the teachers and librarians who have championed my work, to the booksellers (especially the independent ones) who have talked about my books and ensured they are on shelves, and to you, the readers, for spending time with my stories. I couldn't do this job I love without your support, so thank you!

I would be remiss if I didn't take a moment to thank the veterans who have served our country with courage and honor. You have inspired me, and I was able to write this book because you have helped preserve our freedom. Veterans make sacrifices, many unseen, and I want you to know I see you. I would also like to acknowledge the families of veterans. You, too, have made concessions and are often the unsung heroes, facing the consequences of war long after it's over. Thank you for all that you do.

A heartfelt thanks to my mom, who taught me the value of a diverse society and for encouraging me to find my voice and speak up for what's right. Thank you also for your vulnerability in sharing stories of what it was like to grow up with a father in an era when veterans weren't supposed to talk about the trauma they'd endured. I'm truly blessed to have you in my life, and love that we get to talk books on an almost weekly basis.

To Madeline, thank you for reading early chapters of this book, helping me to hone Rebel's voice, and catching details that didn't need to be there. ;) Thank you also for cooking dinner when I was too caught up in the story to stop (which was a lot this time, I'm afraid). I'm so grateful for your continued support and encouragement, your dry wit and intelligence, but most of all, I'm honored to witness the wonderful person you are and that you're becoming.

Finally, thank you to Shane. I don't know what I did to get so lucky to have you in my life, but I'm so glad I do. Thank you for your patience as my mind wanders mid-conversation, for helping with travel arrangements when I suddenly need to go to some obscure location for research, and for all of your support in doing this weird thing I love. Also, a special thanks for our time in Italy. It was just the break I needed to help me power through to the end of this book. Here's to twenty years and counting!

Discussion Guide for
The Inside Battle by Melanie Sumrow

- At the beginning of the book, the author provides an inspirational quote from Dr. Martin Luther King, Jr.: "In the end, we will remember not the words of our enemies, but the silence of our friends." What does this quote mean to you?

- Why do you think it is so hard for Rebel to stand up to his dad, even when he thinks his dad is wrong?

- Do you think Rebel has a right to be angry with Ajeet after the competition? Why or why not?

- Did it surprise you that there were other kids at the training camp? Why or why not?

- The Flag Bearers believe in several anti-government conspiracies. Do you think their beliefs justify their behavior? Why or why not?

- Why do you think Rebel can assemble the weapons, even though he doesn't want to fire them?

- Why do you think Calliope is important to the story?

- Nathan and Josiah are both combat veterans. What do you think makes them different from each other? How are they alike?

- The honeybee is an important symbol used throughout the book. Why do you think the author chose to use the honeybee?

- Josiah "takes a stand" against the Flag Bearers in his own way. Do you agree with his approach? Why or why not?

- At the end of the book, do you think Ajeet should forgive Rebel? Why or why not?

- Do you think Rebel should forgive his dad? Why or why not?